"It's still the most powerful feeling I've ever experienced. And I want to act on it. Now. With you," Tess replied.

"Even though you're scared out of your wits," Cade stated.

Again she swallowed, the muscles moving in her throat. "Guess so."

"So you agree to all my terms? Fidelity, no commitment, and when the time comes a good, clean ending?"

"Are you always this cold-blooded?"

"Yes," he said. "I am. Saves trouble in the long run."

"All right, I agree," she said in a smothered voice.

"Then what are we waiting for?"

Although born in England, **Sandra Field** has lived most of her life in Canada; she says the silence and emptiness of the north speak to her particularly. While she enjoys travelling, and passing on her sense of a new place, she often chooses to write about the city which is now her home. Sandra says, 'I write out of my experience; I have learned that love, with its joys and its pains, is all-important. I hope this knowledge enriches my writing, and touches a chord in you, the reader.'

Recent titles by the same author:

THE MILLIONAIRE'S PREGNANT WIFE
THE JET-SET SEDUCTION
HIS ONE-NIGHT MISTRESS
THE ENGLISH ARISTOCRAT'S BRIDE

THE BILLIONAIRE'S VIRGIN MISTRESS

BY
SANDRA FIELD

MILLS & BOON™
Pure reading pleasure

First published in Great Britain 2008
Harlequin Mills & Boon Limited,
Eton House, 18-24 Paradise Road, Richmond, Surrey TW9 1SR

© Sandra Field 2008

ISBN: 978 0 263 86428 1

Set in Times Roman 10½ on 12¾ pt
01-0508-50711

Printed and bound in Spain
by Litografia Rosés, S.A., Barcelona

THE
BILLIONAIRE'S
VIRGIN MISTRESS

CHAPTER ONE

As THE Malagash Island ferry eased into the dock, Cade Lorimer turned on the ignition of his beloved Maserati and prepared himself for what would undoubtedly be an unpleasant interview.

Saluting the ferry attendant, he drove up the metal ramp onto the narrow highway. He knew exactly where he was going. He owned most of the island, after all. An island now awash in early September sunlight, its thickets of evergreens hugging the cliffs, the sea sparkling as it dashed itself against the rocks.

He was here at the request of Del, his adoptive father. Here on a fool's errand, one that could lead to nothing but trouble—because the woman he was to track down was, in theory, Del's granddaughter.

Del's granddaughter? That had to be the joke of the century. She was a fake. Of course she was.

According to Del she'd been born in Madrid, and had spent most of her life in Europe. Yet for the last eleven months she'd been living a mere forty miles from Del's summer mansion on the coast of Maine.

Cade didn't believe in coincidence. Tess Ritchie was an imposter who'd heard of Del's considerable fortune and was biding her time to lay claim to it.

So it was up to him to stop her. And stop her he would.

On the meadows above the road, three deer were peacefully grazing; Cade's eyes flicked over them, barely registering their presence. Del—so he'd said—had known about Tess ever since she was born, had supported her financially for her entire life, but had never been in touch with her directly or breathed a word about her existence to anyone.

Through local gossip, Cade had long ago found out about Del's biological son, Cory, the black sheep of the family who was, supposedly, Tess Ritchie's father. Del had never breathed a word about Cory's existence, either.

The two best kept secrets on the eastern seaboard, Cade thought, his fingers drumming the soft leather on the steering wheel. If by any chance Tess Ritchie wasn't a fake, then she was related to Del by blood. As he, Cade, was not.

This simple fact rankled; he resented even the possibility of Del having a granddaughter. Stupid of him, no doubt. But wasn't his reaction one more indication of how he'd always felt cheated of any true connection to Del?

Cade rolled down the window, the breeze tugging at his hair. Another minute or two and he'd be there. The investigator's report had stated that Tess Ritchie was renting a converted fish shack just past the village.

The investigator was one Cade himself had used; his reputation was impeccable. But this time, he was out to lunch.

As for strategy, Cade figured he'd wing it once he was face-to-face with Tess Ritchie. For sure, he'd have to fight her off. The woman wasn't born who could resist Del's money, let alone Cade's far more substantial wealth. Billionaire had a certain ring, he had to admit.

So there were two rich men in the family. Yeah, he'd have to fight her off.

He rounded a corner, and there, on the shore of the cove, was a fish shack that had been turned into a small winterized cabin. An image of Moorings, Del's summer place, flashed across Cade's mind; Del wanted him to bring Tess Ritchie to Moorings on the return trip. The contrast with the fish shack was so laughable that Cade's anger jumped another notch.

He turned down the dirt track to the cabin. No car parked outside and no sign of life. Tess Ritchie worked full-time, Tuesday to Saturday, at the local library, that much Cade knew; it was why he'd arrived well before nine on a Saturday morning.

He drew up outside the cabin and climbed out of his car. Waves murmured on the shingled beach; a pair of gulls soared overhead, their wings limned in light. Filling his lungs with cool salt air, Cade briefly forgot his errand in a moment of sheer pleasure. His own love of the sea was a rare bond between him and Del.

With an impatient sigh, he strode over to the door—painted an ebullient shade of yellow—knocked hard and knew instinctively that the silence on the other side of the door was the silence of emptiness. Fool's errand, indeed. She wasn't even home.

On ponderous gray wings a heron flew past; and to Cade's ears came the rattle of footsteps on the pebbles. Swiftly he circled the cabin. A woman wearing brief shorts and a tank top was jogging toward him along the crest of the beach. She was agile, tanned and lithe, her hair jammed under a vivid orange baseball cap.

Then she caught sight of him. She stopped dead in her tracks, her breast heaving from exertion, and for the space of ten full seconds they stared at each other across the expanse of pebbled beach.

At a much slower pace, which was imbued with reluctance—or was it fear? Cade wondered—she started toward him.

On his way to the cabin, he'd pictured a bleached blonde with a slash of red lipstick and a lush, in-your-face body. He'd been wrong. About as wrong as he could be. His mouth dry, his eyes intent, he watched her come to a halt twenty feet away from him, her back to the sun.

No lipstick. A sheen of sweat on her face, most of which was shadowed by the oversize brim of her cap. Workmanlike sneakers on her feet, and legs to die for. He stepped closer and saw her, almost imperceptibly, shrink away from him. She said sharply, "Are you lost? The village is back that way."

"Are you Tess Ritchie?"

"Yes."

"My name's Cade Lorimer. I need to talk to you."

He could easily have missed the tiny flicker of response that crossed her features as he said his name, so swift was it, and as swiftly subdued. Oh, yes, he thought, you're good. Just not quite good enough.

"I'm sorry," she said, not sounding at all sorry, "I don't know you and I don't have the time to talk to you—I need to get ready for work."

"I think, when you know why I'm here, you'll make the time," he said softly.

"Then you think wrong. If you really want to see me, come to the public library. Half a mile down the road, across from the post office. I'll be there until five this afternoon. And now if you'll excuse me—"

"Lorimer," Cade said. "The name doesn't ring a bell?"

"Why should it?"

"Del Lorimer is my father—he's the one who sent me here. His other son—Cory—was your father."

Her body went rigid. In a staccato voice, she said, "How do you know my father's name?"

"Let's go inside. As I said, we have things to talk about."

But she was backing away, step by step, her gaze glued to his face. "I'm not going anywhere with you," she said, her fists clenched by her side so tightly that the knuckles were white.

Terror, Cade thought, puzzled. Why the hell would she be terrified of him? She should be jumping up and down for joy that Del Lorimer had finally sent someone to seek her out. "If you don't want to go inside," he said, "we can talk out here. There's lots of time—the library doesn't open for an hour and a half."

"Talk about what?"

"Your grandfather. Wendel—better know as Del—Lorimer. Who just happens to spend his summers forty miles down the coast. Don't tell me you don't know about him because I won't believe you."

"You're out of your mind," she whispered. "I don't have a grandfather. My grandparents died years ago—not that that's any of your business. Whatever your game is, Mr. Lorimer, I don't like it. Please leave. And don't come back, or I'll set the police on you."

The sheriff on Malagash Island was a longtime friend of Cade's. He should have come up with a strategy, Cade thought irritably, because this wasn't going the way he'd imagined it would. "Who told you your grandparents died?"

A tiny shiver rippled through her body; she hugged her arms to her chest. "Go away—just leave me alone."

"We have several options here, but that's not one of them." Cade's jaw tightened. Above her thin tank top, he could see the enticing shadow of her cleavage. Her arms were smoothly muscled, her fingers long and narrow. Ringless, he noticed, and in a sudden spurt of rage recalled the Lorimer family diamonds.

He'd had enough of this ridiculous fencing. In a blur of movement, he closed the distance between them, gripped her by the arms and said forcefully, "Your grandfather sent me. Cory Lorimer's father."

Ducking her head, she kicked out at him, as vicious and unexpected as a snake. As Cade automatically evaded the slash of her foot, she tore free and took off at a run up the slope.

In five fast strides, Cade caught up with her, grabbed her by the shoulder and tugged her around to face him. But before he could say anything, her body went limp in his hold. Oh, yeah, he thought cynically, oldest trick in the book. Digging his fingers into her shoulder because she was a dead weight, he wrapped the other arm around her waist.

Then, to his dismay, he realized it wasn't a trick. She'd fainted, a genuine, no-fooling faint. Face paper-white, eyes shut, body boneless. With a muttered curse, he lowered her to the ground and thrust her head between her knees.

So the terror had been real. What in God's name was going on? Impulsively he pulled the ball cap off her head, loosing a tumble of dark chestnut curls from which the sun teased streaks of gold. It was soft between his fingers, silky smooth. She was too thin, he thought. But her skin was like silk, too.

Then she stirred, muttering something under her breath. He said with a calmness he was far from feeling, "I'm sorry—I shouldn't have frightened you like that."

He could hear her trying to steady her breath; the small sounds smote him with compunction. He added, "I've never in my life terrified a woman into fainting—not my style. Which is something you'll have to take on trust. Look, let's start again. I have a very important message for you, one I've promised to deliver. But we can do this outside, so you'll feel safe."

Slowly Tess raised her head, her hair falling around her face. She needed a haircut, she thought distantly. Time to get out the scissors and hack the ends off.

The man was still there. Through her tumbled curls she saw hair black as the ravens that flocked the beaches, eyes the harsh gray of the cliffs that ringed the island. His face was carved like the cliffs—hard, unyielding, craggy. And undeniably, terrifyingly male.

A stranger. But worse than a stranger, she thought with a superstitious shiver. Her fate. Dark, dangerous and full of secrets.

Pushing her hair back, terror rising in her throat again so that she could scarcely breathe, she said raggedly, "I've nothing here worth stealing. No money, and I don't do drugs, I swear I don't."

Cade Lorimer said blankly, "Your eyes. They're green."

Panic-stricken, she gaped at him. Con artist, or certifiably mad? What did green eyes have to do with anything? She pushed hard against him and said frantically, "There's nothing here for you. Cory's dead—he's been dead for years. Can't you just leave me in peace?"

Cade's heart was thudding in his chest; her words scarcely registered. In all his life, he'd only known one other person with eyes that true, deep green, the green of wet leaves in springtime. That person was Del Lorimer.

She must be Del's granddaughter. She had to be. "Do you wear contact lenses?" he rapped.

Temper streaked with a flash of humor came to her rescue, briefly subduing fear. "Which mental ward have you escaped from? You're here to rob me and you want to know if I wear contacts?"

"Just answer me," Cade said brusquely. "Your eyes—are they really green?"

"Of course they are—what sort of stupid question is that?"

"The only question that matters," he said heavily. So she wasn't a fake; he'd been way off base. That wasn't his style, either.

As for her, her whole body was taut with tension; she was looking at him as warily as if he really was an escapee from a mental institution. Or a thief, the other accusation she'd thrown at him.

Logically he should explain the significance of her eye color. But he wasn't quite ready to do that. "I'm no thief—I have all the money I need," Cade said, "and I'm entirely sane. As for drugs, I've never touched them—more than enough excitement in day-to-day living without dosing myself with chemical additives." He hesitated, then added with huge reluctance, "I'm here to give you something, not to take anything away."

"There's nothing you can give me that I would want," she said stonily. "Nothing."

"How can you say that, when you haven't heard me out?" His smile didn't reach his eyes. "The first step is for both of us to stand up, how about it?"

He took her by the elbow. The coolness of her skin seeped into his pores; her nearness sent heat licking along his veins, liquid heat, primitive and lethal. Oh, no, he thought, appalled. He wasn't going to lust after Del's granddaughter. That really wasn't in the cards.

But as he eased her upright, his senses were assaulted by her body's fragility, and by the scent of lavender, delicate and uncomplicated, that drifted from her skin. Again desire ravaged him, unasked for, totally unwelcome. With all the willpower at his command, a willpower honed over the years, Cade kept his face an unrevealing mask and forced himself to relax.

Shrugging off his fleece vest, he wrapped it around her shoulders. "You're cold," he said. "Go inside and get something warm on. You could call the police, too—Dan Pollard's the sheriff's name, I've known him for years. Give him a description, and he'll vet me. Then we'll talk."

Tess swallowed. Cade Lorimer was standing too close to her, much too close. But while there was concern in his voice, and remorse overlying the gray depths of his gaze, she had the strong sense that both these emotions were, at best, superficial. Lorimer, she thought, and shuddered. How could she trust anyone with the same last name as Cory, her father? "I'll call the police right away," she said flatly. "Don't follow me into the house."

A gull screamed overhead as she walked steadily toward the cabin. The door shut decisively behind her, and Cade heard the snap of the lock. Restlessly he began prowling up and down. If she really was Del's granddaughter, why had she never contacted Del? She'd been here for nearly a year, and not once had she put the touch on him. So what kind of game was she playing? Lying to him, telling him both her grandparents were dead, acting as though he, Cade, was a combination of Attila the Hun and Hannibal Lector.

What was taking her so long?

Swiftly he walked around the back of the cabin, wondering if he'd fallen for the second oldest trick in the book—escape via the back door. But through the plate glass windows that overlooked a small deck and the ocean, he could see Tess Ritchie inside the cabin, her back to him as she did something at the stove. Declining to spy on her, Cade turned and stared out to sea.

No answers there.

The back door scraped open. Tess said, "I've made coffee. I'll give you sixteen minutes of my time and not a minute more."

"Did you phone the sheriff?"

As she gave a choppy nod, Cade pulled up one of the cheap plastic chairs and sat down. She set a tray on the low table. Her movements swift, she poured two mugs of steaming coffee and pushed a plate of muffins toward him. "Home-made?" he asked casually.

"Blueberry. I picked the berries two weeks ago. I've lived here nearly a year—why did you pick today to turn up?"

He knew exactly how long she'd lived here. "A month ago my grandfather had a minor heart attack. It scared the pants off him—his first intimation that he, like everyone else, is mortal. That's when he hired an investigator to—"

"An investigator?"

The terror was back, full force, nor was she making any effort to mask it. "That's right," Cade said, all his suspicions resurfacing. "Del wanted to discover your whereabouts. Eventually the investigator came up with this location. You must have known of Del's existence, or why else would you be living so close?"

Tess buried her nose in her mug, inhaling the pungency of the dark Colombian blend. "I'm living on the island because I was offered a job here and I love the sea." And because, she thought, it was a very long way from Amsterdam. "Why would Cory lie, telling me both my grandparents were dead?" she flashed. "My grandfather died years ago, in New York City. Not long after, my grandmother succumbed to pneumonia."

"Was Cory a truthful man?"

Her fingers tightened around the handle of her mug. "He had no reason to lie."

"He did lie. Del's very much alive and wants to meet you. That's why I'm here—to bring that about."

Coffee sloshed over the rim of her mug. "No."

"You haven't even heard me out."

"I don't want to meet him! Ever. Go home and tell him that, and don't either of you bother me again."

"That's not good enough."

"Maybe you should try looking at it from my point of view," she snapped, color flagging her cheeks.

Cade looked at her in silence. Her cheekbones flared like wings; her lips were a soft and voluptuous curve, infinitely enticing, while her eyes, so exotically shaped, so vivid in hue, drew him like a magnet. She was—he knew this without a shadow of doubt—the most beautiful woman he'd ever seen.

He'd seen—and bedded—more than a few beautiful women.

"So what is your point of view?" he said in a hard voice.

Fractionally she hesitated. "I disliked my father," she said evenly. "Disliked and distrusted him. I therefore have no wish to meet his father—a man who, let's be frank, has ignored my existence for twenty-two years."

Cade leaned forward, clipping off his words. "He's supported you financially for twenty-two years. Or are you forgetting that?"

She gave an incredulous laugh. "Supported me? Are you kidding?"

"Every month of your life, money's been deposited in a Swiss account for your use."

She banged her mug on the table; more coffee spilled over the rim. "You're lying—I've never seen a penny of that money."

"Or are you lying?" Cade said with dangerous softness. "There's a lot more money where that came from."

She surged to her feet. "Don't insult me—I wouldn't touch Lorimer money! It's the last thing I need."

Cade stood up, too, and deliberately let his gaze wander over the plastic furniture and the roughly shingled walls of the little cabin. "Doesn't look that way to me."

"Money," she spat, "you think it can buy everything? Look around you, Cade Lorimer. I go to sleep at night to the sound of the waves. I watch the tides come and go, the shorebirds feed, the deer wander over the hill. I'm free here, I'm in control of my own life and I'm finally learning to be happy—and no one's going to take that from me. No one! Including Del Lorimer."

Abruptly Tess ran out of words. Dammit, she thought, why did I spout off like that? I never talk about myself to anyone. And then to bare my soul to Cade Lorimer, of all people. A man who screams danger from every pore.

He was watching her, those storm-gray eyes focused on her, intent as a hunter who sees movement in the underbrush. "One of us is lying," he said, "and it isn't me."

"Then why are you so anxious to introduce me to my grandfather?" she said sweetly, "if I'm nothing but a money-grubbing liar?"

"Because he asked me to."

"Oh, so you dance to his tune? But of course, I'm forgetting, he's a very rich man."

Cade's breath hissed between his teeth. Had he ever known a woman to get so easily under his skin? "Del gave me a secure and happy childhood," he grated, "and taught me a great deal over the years. Now he's old and he's sick, and it's payback time."

Tess said, going on intuition, "You didn't mean to tell me that, did you? Any more that I meant to sound off about freedom and happiness."

Infuriated by her accuracy, Cade picked up his mug and drained it. "You make a mean cup of coffee, Tess Ritchie," he said with a wolfish grin. "In your lunch hour, go on the Internet and look up Lorimer Inc.—check me and Del out, get a few facts. I'm taking you out for dinner after work. I'll pick you up here, sharp at six-thirty, and we'll continue this conversation."

She raised brows as elegant as wings. "Are you giving me orders?"

"You catch on fast."

"I have my faults, but stupidity isn't among them."

"I didn't think it was," he said dryly.

"Good. Then you'll understand why I'm not going out for dinner with you. Goodbye, Mr. Lorimer. It's been…interesting."

"So interesting that I'm not about to say goodbye. Come off it, Tess—you're certainly smart enough to know I won't vanish just because it suits you. Six-thirty. If nothing else, you'll get a free meal at the hotel, prepared by one of the finest chefs along the coast." His smile bared his teeth. "Besides, I've been told I'm a passable dinner date. Now hadn't you better get ready for work instead of standing there staring at me with your mouth open? I wouldn't want you to be late."

"I'm not—"

He took the two steps off the deck in a single stride, loped around the corner of the cabin, got in his car and roared up the slope.

He'd gotten away from her without touching her again. For which he deserved a medal. And he knew exactly what he was going to do next. A self-imposed task, the potential results rather more important than he liked.

CHAPTER TWO

CAREFULLY Cade steered the Maserati between the potholes in Tess's driveway. He was twenty-five minutes early. Only, he assured himself, because he'd completed his task, and the paperback novel he'd brought with him had failed to hold his attention.

Nothing to do with Tess, and the itch under his skin to see her again.

He climbed out of his car and knocked on her door. No answer. He knocked again, feeling his nerves tighten. Had he been a fool to take her for granted, and assume she'd be meekly waiting for him? She was no pushover. If she didn't want to see him again, she'd take measures to put that into effect.

He tried the door, which, to his surprise, opened smoothly. Stepping inside, he closed it behind him. Ella Fitzgerald was crooning on the stereo; the shower was running full-blast.

Tess was home. She hadn't run away.

It shouldn't matter to him as much as it did.

Cade looked around, taking his time. Clothes were flung over the chair: a black dress, hose and sleek black underwear that raised his blood pressure a full notch. Dragging his eyes away, he took in the cheerful hooked rugs dotting the worn pineboard floor, and an array of cushions that brightened the sagging chesterfield. Books overflowed the homemade shelves. The room was spotlessly clean.

Absolutely no evidence that she'd ever had any access to Del's allowance, or to any other substantial source of money, Cade thought. Basically it was the room of someone who lived off a minimal paycheck.

Someone who'd be far from immune to the Lorimers' wealth.

The CD came to an end. He flipped through a stack of discs, discovering old favorites of his own, intrigued by how eclectic a collection it was. He selected a CD and snapped open the cover.

The shower shut off. As he leaned down to push the play button, a door opened behind him and he heard the soft pad of bare feet on the wooden floor. He turned around.

Tess shrieked with alarm, clutching the towel to her breasts. Her hair was wrapped in another towel, turban-fashion, emphasizing her slender throat and those astonishing cheekbones; her shoulders were pearled with water and her legs went on forever. He wanted her, Cade thought. Wanted her here and now. Fiercely and without any thought for the consequences.

He wasn't going to do a damn thing about it. For starters, she was Del's granddaughter and strictly off-limits. Plus— more importantly—he was far from convinced she was as innocent as she looked. Too much money was at stake.

She said shakily, "You're early."

"I did knock. The door wasn't locked."

"I usually don't bother locking it. Although I guess I should when you're around."

He said hoarsely, "Tess—"

"Don't come near me!"

The terror was back full force. "Sometime—soon—you're going to tell me why I frighten you so badly," he said. "I made a dinner reservation for seven—charming though you look right now, a towel won't cut it."

Her heart was still racketing in her chest. Sure, he'd startled her. But it was more than that. In his light gray suit, blue shirt and silk tie, Cade looked formidably sophisticated and wholly, disturbingly male. Not to mention sexy, a word she avoided like the plague.

She was the nearest thing to naked.

Power, she thought slowly, that's what he breathed; although he was quite possibly unaware of it. Power. Money. Sexual charisma. All three put his danger quotient off the chart.

She didn't do sex.

To her horror, she heard herself blurt, "If Del Lorimer's my grandfather, that makes you my uncle." This all-too-obvious fact hadn't struck her until five minutes after Cade had driven away from her cabin this morning.

"I'm Del's adopted son," Cade said curtly. "No blood relation to your grandfather at all. Or to you." Just as well, he thought savagely, given the way his hormones were acting up.

Adopted. Not a blood relative. But not her fate, either, Tess thought in a sudden snap of fury. Merely a man who was a total stranger to her, and who would remain just that—a stranger.

Unfortunately her thoughts didn't stop there. Because she'd grown up in an environment where she could trust nothing, she'd always endeavored to remain honest with herself. If she were to be honest now, relief had been her predominant emotion that Cade Lorimer wasn't related to her by blood; close on its heels had been utter dismay at all the implications of that relief.

It didn't matter who Cade was. She just didn't do sex.

Deeply grateful he couldn't read her mind, she said tartly, "So you're an adopted son. If I'm the newly discovered grand-daughter, aren't you afraid I'll supplant you?"

"No," Cade said coldly, and watched her lower her lashes, her face unreadable.

Then she looked up, meeting his gaze in unspoken challenge. "My clothes are on the chair," she said. "Turn your back."

Unwillingly admiring her spirit, he tore his eyes from the silken slopes of her bare shoulders and did as she asked. "You okay with this music?"

"Meatloaf, Verdi, Diana Krall," she said wildly, "play what you like. And I'm not wearing a towel for dinner, I'm wearing a dress. The only one I own, so if it's not up to your standards, too bad."

"You'd look gorgeous wearing burlap."

"Mr. Cade Flattery Lorimer," she retorted, picking up her clothes and holding them like a shield in front of her.

Suddenly angry, Cade turned to face her. "I mean it. Look in the mirror, for God's sake—you're an extraordinarily beautiful woman."

Her jaw dropped. "I'm too skinny and my hair's a mess."

He grinned at her, a mocking grin sparked with so much energy that it took her breath away. "Slender, not skinny," he drawled. "Although you're right about the hair—a good cut would do wonders."

"What *is* your angle? If money doesn't work, try sex?"

"What a wildcat you are. Hissing and spitting if anyone gets near you."

"Whereas you're like a panther! Sleek and dangerous."

She hadn't meant to say that. Only to think it.

"Now who's pouring on the flattery?" Cade said. "Get dressed and dry that mop of hair, or we'll be late for dinner."

Oddly enough, beneath a storm of emotions she couldn't possibly have labeled, Tess was very hungry. Scowling, she marched out of the room with as much dignity as she could muster when swathed in an old blue bath towel, and shut her bedroom door with more than necessary force. For the first time in her life, she wished she owned a real dress. Something out of *Vogue*, stunningly simple, reeking of money and sophistication.

With a vicious snap she switched on her hair dryer. She didn't have time to cut her hair, but she was going to slather on eye shadow and mascara. For courage, she thought, picking up her brush.

Because wasn't one of the several reasons she'd decided to keep this dinner date the simple fact that running away was the coward's way out?

In the last few years, she'd done too much running.

Cade had put on Mozart by the time Tess walked back into the living room. Taking his time, he looked her up and down, noticing instantly that her fingernails were digging into her palms, and her jaw was tight. Her dress was a plain black sheath, teamed with sheer black hose and stiletto heels. She'd swept her tangle of hair into a knot high on her head; clustered black beads dangled from her earlobes. Her mouth—his own went dry—was a luscious raspberry-red. He said, "Beautiful's such an overused word—you take my breath away."

Her heart lurched in her breast. She said coolly, "I made my dress from a remnant that was on sale. The shoes come from Second Time Around—I only hope the original owner won't be eating dinner at the hotel."

"I bet she never looked that good in them."

"You're too kind."

Part of her liked this verbal banter, Tess thought uneasily. Quelling a stab of fear, she took a white mohair sweater from the cupboard, flung it around her shoulders and stalked out the door.

Cade's car smelled of leather; he drove with smooth competence, making small talk about the scenery. Ten minutes later they were seated in the hotel dining room by a window overlooking the ocean, the applewood in the fireplace crackling cheerfully. Trying not to panic at the alarming array of silverware, Tess took a deep breath and went on the offensive. "Your company—Lorimer Inc.—owns this hotel. And many others, worldwide, all part of the DelMer chain of fine hotels."

"Del has rather a large ego—he liked the idea of combining his two names. So you checked him out."

"Him and his adopted son. I'd be a fool not to meet him, wouldn't I? A rich old man—every woman's dream."

"No more shoes from Second Time Around," Cade said.

"No more hose from the dollar store." The waiter put a menu in front of her, a thick leather binder embossed with gold. She wasn't going to be intimidated by a menu, Tess thought resolutely, and opened it to the first page. "Once I've hooked up with Del, I could buy the dollar store. A whole string of them."

"You could," Cade said. "Do you like martinis?"

She'd never had one. "Of course."

"Straight up or on the rocks?"

"On the rocks. I could buy a car like yours."

"Several, I should think."

Her eyes narrowed. She was doing her best to act like the crassest of fortune-hunters, and Cade wasn't even reacting. If anything, he was laughing at her. Chewing on her lip, she added, "I'd inherit a ton of money when my grandfather dies. Enough to buy diamond earrings and go on a world cruise."

"Lorimer Inc. owns a fleet of cruise ships—you could take your pick. Stateroom, the works. I'm sure by then you'd have found some diamonds to your taste."

She'd never liked the look of diamonds. Too cold, too flashy. "Emeralds, to go with my eyes," she said dreamily.

"Excellent choice…have you decided on an appetizer?"

The menu was in Italian with the English in script below. When she was eleven, she'd spent a year in Rome with Cory and Opal, her wayward mother; Tess said in impeccable Italian, "I'll have *fegato grasso al mango*." She flipped the page. "With *stufato di pesce* for a main course."

Each was the most expensive item on the page. Blanking out the actual dollar amount, she said with as much innuendo as her conscience would allow, "How is your grandfather's health? You mentioned a heart attack."

"Oh, I suspect he's got a good many years in him yet. You might have to wait for that inheritance."

"Or is the inheritance like the support—nonexistent?" she retorted. "If, as you claim, I really am related to him, I could always go to the press. Illegitimate Granddaughter Cheated Of Her Rights—I can see the headlines now, can't you?"

With a flourish, the waiter put the martinis on the table, and took their orders. Tess loathed olives. She picked up the frosted glass and took a hefty swallow. Her face convulsed. "That's straight antifreeze!"

"Your first martini?" Cade said innocently.

"They don't serve them at the chicken takeout." She grimaced. "I see why—who'd want to eat olives pickled in ethylene glycol?"

Cade signaled the waiter, asked for a brandy Alexander, and said smoothly, "Del hates martinis, too. And loves the ocean."

"Does he? How nice. You know, if allegedly he's been supporting me since I was born, he owes me quite a backlog." She smiled at Cade, batting her mascaraed lashes. "I'd better hire a good lawyer."

"It would have to be a very good one to take on Lorimer Inc."

"Then there's you," she said in a voice like cream, brushing his fingers with her own, letting them linger until every nerve in his body tightened. "You make Del's fortune look like small change."

It was the first time she'd touched him voluntarily; and how he loathed her motive for doing it. Holding tight to his temper, Cade watched her pout her raspberry-red lips, heard her purr, "I'd be a fool to turn my back on you or Del, Cade. But especially you."

His voice taut, because there was a limit to what a man had to put up with, Cade said, "Do you want to know what I did today? I wandered around the village talking to people about you. People who've known you for the better part of eleven months." The pout was gone, he noticed with mean pleasure, replaced by blank shock. Calmly he kept going. "I'm sure you'd agree with me that the islanders to a man—or woman— are sober New Englanders who don't go in for flattery. They described you as reliable, honest, frugal, hardworking. Likes to walk the beaches by herself. Hardly ever goes off-island. No friends. No wild parties. No men."

Tess gripped the edge of the table. "You spent the day *gossiping* about me? How dare you! And why would they talk to *you*? The islanders aren't just sober, they're closemouthed to a fault."

"Several years ago, I paid top dollar to buy up ninety percent of the island. Made it into a nature conservancy to protect it from development—the only concession being that I build this place." Cade waved his martini at his surroundings. "So I'm in like a dirty sock—the islanders love me. You might as well drop the gold-digger act, it's wasted on me. You can't fool an islander— if they say you're honest as the tide turns, I'll go along with that."

For now, he added silently.

With exquisite timing, the waiter deposited a creamy drink sprinkled with nutmeg in front of her. She glared at it, trying to gather her wits. She'd just made a total fool of herself. Good job, Tess. What's the follow-up?

"Try your drink," Cade said, giving her the full benefit of his smile. One of his women had called it lethal; another, dynamite. It was a weapon he wasn't above using when it suited him.

But instead of blushing in confusion or smiling back, Tess said furiously, "I've never laid eyes on one red cent of your grandfather's money."

His smile faded. "That was the next item on my agenda." He waited while her antipasto was put in front of her. "I talked to Del today. He's a stubborn, cantankerous old man, who likes control and claims he's mislaid the investigator's report—"

"You haven't seen it?"

The emotion in her face was unquestionably relief. Cade picked up his fork. "No. But I did get out of Del—by sheer bloody-mindedness—the investigator's discovery that ever since your father died six years ago, your allowance has been siphoned off the account by your mother. Opal Ritchie. I can only presume Cory took it prior to that."

Briefly Tess shut her eyes. Opal and Cory. Her parents. Cory with his unpredictable rages, his drug-induced highs. Opal, wild, willful, never to be trusted. The rooms, she thought. Oh God, those awful rooms…

"What's wrong?" Cade demanded.

When she opened her eyes, she was back in the elegant dining room, with its high-arched windows and vaulted ceiling, its polite murmur of conversation; and a pair of stormy-gray eyes boring into her soul. "I'm fine," she said flatly, and with superhuman effort pulled herself together. The brandy Alexander, which was delicious, slid down her throat. The array of silver looked a little less intimidating. Carefully she selected the mate of the fork Cade had used and took a bite of mango, chewing thoroughly, tasting nothing. "You called me a liar back at the cabin."

"I shouldn't have doubted you," Cade said curtly. At least with regard to Del's monthly support, he shouldn't have. But he still had plenty of other questions about the all-too-desirable and highly enigmatic Tess Ritchie.

The tight knot in her chest easing somewhat—for hadn't he more or less apologized?—Tess said shrewdly, "You still wish I was a thousand miles away from Del, don't you? So you and I are on the same wavelength. The distance'll be forty miles, not a thousand—but forty miles is plenty. Because I don't care about the Lorimer money. His or yours. I like my life here on the island, it's all I want and I'm not leaving here. You can tell my grandfather I'm grateful he did his best to support me—it wasn't his fault that I never saw the money. But it's too late now. I don't need his support anymore."

Her green eyes blazed with honesty. Disconcerted, Cade discovered in himself a contrary and ridiculous urge to take her words at face value. To trust her.

He'd never trusted a woman in his life other than Selena, his mother, whose every motive had been on the surface for all to see. Tess wasn't Selena. Tess was mysterious, fiery and unpredictable.

Trust her? He'd be a fool to be betrayed by a pair of emerald-green eyes.

He'd been holding a weapon in abeyance. Deciding now was the time to use it, Cade said coolly, "Del told me something else today—that the investigator drew a complete blank for the year you turned sixteen. The year your father died. What happened that year?"

Her skin went cold. A roaring filled her ears. She couldn't faint again, she thought desperately. Not twice in one day. She shoved the fork in her mouth, and concentrated on chewing. She might as well have been eating cardboard.

She'd slept wrapped in cardboard for over two months.

Forcing herself to swallow, desperate to change the subject, she said jaggedly, "Where does my grandfather spend his winters?"

Cade sat back in his chair, gazing at her, his brain in overdrive. Mysterious was a euphemism where Tess was concerned. She was secretive and closemouthed, a woman for whom terror was a constant companion. What had she done at sixteen—or what had happened to her—to induce that blank-eyed stare, those trembling fingers?

He shoved down an unwelcome pang of compassion, allowing all his latent distrust to rise to the surface instead. She'd been a model of good behavior ever since she'd arrived on Malagash Island. But preceding that? What then?

"Are you in trouble with the law?" he demanded.

"No," she said. But her gaze was downcast, and her voice lacked conviction.

Fine, he thought. I might just do some investigating on my own behalf. Del likes to think he holds the reins, but I'm the one in control here.

With equal certainty Cade knew that if he didn't bring Tess Ritchie back to Moorings, Del would order the chauffeur to drive him to the island and find her for himself.

He said casually, "You speak very good Italian."

"When I was twelve, I lived for a year in Rome." She glanced up, her eyes shuttered. "I also speak German, Dutch, French and a smattering of Spanish. A European upbringing has its advantages." Which, she thought bitterly, really was lying.

"Favorite artist?"

"Van Gogh. I don't see how anyone could live in Amsterdam and not love his work. Rembrandt and Vermeer close seconds."

"Your tastes in music are eclectic and you like espionage novels."

"You should be the investigator," she said nastily. "I also like medieval art, lavender soap and pizza with anchovies."

Lavender, he thought, remembering the fragrant, misty rows of blue in the fields of Provence. It was an unsophisticated scent, earthy and real, that somehow suited her. Trying to focus, he said at random, "Which university did you attend?"

Her lashes flickered. She said edgily, "There are other ways of getting an education."

"Where's your mother living now?"

She dropped her fork with a small clatter. "I have no idea."

Her main course was put in front of her. Tess grabbed the nearest knife and fork and started to eat. Red wine had been poured in her glass, the firelight dancing like rubies in its depths. In sudden despair, exhausted by memories she only rarely allowed to surface, she craved to be home in her little cabin, the woodstove burning, a mug of hot chocolate on the table beside her.

And the clock turned back, so that she'd never met Cade Lorimer; never heard of a putative grandfather who lived only forty miles away.

Cade said, "I've upset you."

"You're good at that."

"I'd noticed. I'll book myself into the hotel and get in touch with Del tonight—we'll go see him tomorrow morning. The library's closed Sunday and Monday—I checked."

"I'm sure you did. I'm not going."

No point in arguing now, Cade thought. But at least there was some color back in her cheeks.

What *had* she done at sixteen? Quelling a question he couldn't possibly answer, he began talking about the Vermeers he'd seen at the Metropolitan Museum, segueing to the political scene in Manhattan; and discovered she was well-informed, her judgments acute, occasionally slanted in a way that fascinated him. Then, of course, there was the play of firelight in the thick mass of her hair, the shadows shifting over her delicate collarbone and ivory throat.

Wanting her hadn't gone away; it had, if anything, intensified. Good thing he was known for his willpower; he was going to need all of it. Because to seduce Tess Ritchie would be a very bad move.

They were sipping espressos when his cell phone rang. "Excuse me a minute," he said, and took it from his pocket. "Lorimer," he barked.

Tess straightened her shoulders, trying to work the tension from them unobtrusively. In half an hour she'd be home, her door locked, her life resuming its normal, peaceful pattern.

Peace was all she wanted. Peace, order and control.

Then, abruptly, her attention switched to Cade's side of the conversation. "He's *what*?" Cade was saying. "How bad? So you're at the hospital now. Okay, I'll be on my way in five minutes. I'll see you tomorrow, Doc. Thanks."

He pushed the end button and thrust the phone back in his pocket. The color had drained from his face, his jaw a tight line. He said flatly, "Del's had another heart attack. A minor one, according to his family doctor." He waved to the waiter. "We'll leave as soon as I've paid the bill."

So Cade loves his adoptive father, Tess thought, and felt emotion clog her throat. Cory hadn't loved her. Ever.

She never cried. Couldn't afford to. So why did she feel like crying now? She forced the tears down, watching Cade pass over his credit card.

What if Del Lorimer had another heart attack in the night, and died? She'd never meet him. Never find out if he really was her grandfather, or if this whole farrago was the product of an overeager investigator. But if Del was, by any chance, truly her grandfather, blood of her blood, shouldn't she see him, find out if he was a replica of Cory or someone entirely different?

We…Cade had said a few moments ago. *We'll leave*…she thoroughly disliked the way he'd taken it for granted that she'd go with him.

It was her choice, and only hers.

Stay or go.

CHAPTER THREE

TRYING to decide what she should do, Tess gazed at Cade in silence; he was frowning at the bill, his mind obviously elsewhere. What if he drove off the road because he was thinking about Del rather than his driving?

Somehow the decision had made itself. Tess said evenly, "If I come with you, I'll need some clothes."

"No time," Cade said. "We can get anything you need tomorrow. Let's go."

As obediently as a well-trained hound, she followed him out of the dining room to his car; and felt her heart contract when it took him two attempts to get the key in the ignition. "Are you all right to drive?" she asked.

"Don't worry—I won't put you in the ditch."

It's you I'm worried about, not me. As she fastened her seat belt, the soft leather seat enveloping her, Tess knew her words for the truth. How long since she'd allowed anyone else to matter to her?

Forever and a day.

Or, more accurately, not since that hot summer's night when she was five, and she and her parents had fled Madrid on the midnight train. Just the three of them: they'd left behind

Tess's beloved nanny, Ysabel, without Tess even having the chance to say goodbye to her.

That long-ago heartbreak, so laced with betrayal, had cured Tess, once and for all, of letting anyone close to her.

The last person she should allow to bend that rule was Cade Lorimer. Yet for some reason Tess found herself gazing at his hands, wrapped around the leather-coated steering wheel. Strong hands with a dusting of dark hair, and long, lean fingers that made her ache somewhere deep inside.

She dragged her eyes away, staring out the window. The brief ferry trip was soon over, the forty-mile drive passing in a blur of black spruce, dark rocks and the glitter of the moon on the sea. Although Cade showed no inclination to talk and she had nothing to say, the silence was far from restful. It was a relief when he pulled into the parking lot of an imposing brick building, and she could get out of the car and stretch her legs. "Hospital's state of the art," he said without a trace of emotion, striding toward the entrance. "Del endowed it after my mother died two years ago."

"Oh…I'm sorry she's dead."

"Del's lost without her," Cade said tersely, pushing open the door.

And you, she wondered, did you love your mother just as you so obviously love Del?

Then, to her dismay, Cade took her by the hand. His palm was warm, his fingers clasping hers with automatic strength. With shocking speed, heat raced through her body, fiery and inescapable. Her steps faltered, every nerve on high alert. The ache in her belly intensified, and she could no more deny it than she could shut out the long corridor with its antiseptic smell and polished tile floor. Desire, she thought helplessly

I've never felt it in my life, yet recognize it as though I've always known it. How can that be?

It was more than she could do to pull her hand away. Because Cade needed her, or because she was a total fool?

Desire wasn't on the list, any more than sex.

They'd arrived at the elevator. As they rose to the second floor, Tess stared at the controls, her body a tumult of longing that both terrified and bewildered her. She forced her features to immobility. She couldn't bear for Cade to guess her feelings, for then she would truly be naked in front of him.

As they left the elevator, the nurse on duty smiled at Cade. "Room 204," she said. "He's resting well."

"Thanks," Cade said briefly. Outside the room, he hesitated, inwardly steeling himself for whatever he might find.

Tess tried to tug her hand free. But his fingers tightened, and—short of causing a scene—she had no choice but to follow him into the room. Standing at his side, tension singing along her nerves, Tess looked down at the man in the bed.

Del Lorimer was asleep, his mane of silver hair spread on the pillow, his strongly corded arms bare to the elbow. Automatically she recorded a beak of a nose, an obstinate chin and the facial wrinkles of a man who's lived his life at full tilt.

She felt not the slightest flicker of recognition. Not even remotely did he remind her of Cory.

Swiftly Tess switched her gaze to Cade; and with dismay saw a man closed against any emotion. His features were tight, his jaw clenched, while his eyes were like dark pits, unreadable and unreachable.

In unconscious antipathy she moved away from him so that their shoulders were no longer touching. She'd been wrong: Cade didn't love his adoptive father. By the look of him, love wasn't a word he'd even recognize.

In a way, she was glad to see his true colors so clearly; it made it easier to dismiss him as a ruthless interloper who was interfering in her life with results she could neither anticipate nor desire.

Desire. That word again.

Desire someone incapable of loving the father who—on Cade's own admission—had given him security and love as a boy? She'd have to be crazy to do that.

To her relief, a white-jacketed doctor came to the door. Cade joined him there, holding a low-voiced conversation, then came back into the room. "We might as well go," he said impersonally. "Del will sleep the night through, there's no point in staying."

For a split second Tess looked down at the man lying so still in the bed, a man who, other than common human concern, meant nothing to her. Then she preceded Cade out of the room, walking fast down the hushed, immaculate corridor.

Sixteen minutes after they left the hospital, Cade slowed at two impressive stone pillars and turned down a driveway that wound between stiff Scotch pines and a forest of rhododendrons. Del's stone mansion boasted grandiose white pillars, a formal array of windows and huge chimneys, and equally formal gardens, raked, clipped and weeded to a neatness nature never intended.

Tess disliked it on sight.

For the first time, she broke the silence since they'd left the hospital. "You'll take me home tomorrow," she said.

Cade rubbed his neck, trying to get the tension out. "You can sleep in the west wing," he said. "You'll hear the sea through the windows."

"Tomorrow," she repeated inflexibly.

He shifted in his seat so that he was gazing into her vivid green eyes. Against his will, an image of Del flashed across his mind: a shrunken old man lying too still in a hospital bed, the bars raised on either side. "Give it a rest, Tess," he said sharply. "Haven't we argued enough for one day?"

"Then perhaps you should try listening to me."

Whatever her background, she'd learned to fight for herself, he thought, watching the night shadows slant across her face. Her skin gleamed pale, infinitely desirable, the pulse throbbing gently at the base of her throat. Flooding him as irresistibly as a storm surge, he longed to rest his face there, close his eyes and let the warmth of her skin seep through his pores.

Not since he'd started dating had he ever been pulled so strongly to a woman. It wasn't the way he operated. Easy come, easy go, everything pleasant and on the surface, that was him. He sure as hell wasn't going to break that pattern with Tess Ritchie. Might as well step into a minefield.

Anyway, judging by the look on her face, she'd rather clobber him than hold him close.

"Let's go in," he said, and climbed out of the car.

When he unlocked the massive oak door, four large dogs came scrabbling across the marble floor, barking in excitement, white teeth gleaming. With a gasp of pure horror, Tess grabbed Cade, thrusting him between her and the dogs. *The alley, the dog snarling…crack of a gunshot.*

"Down!" Cade said, and all four subsided, jaws agape, tongues lolling. Swiftly he turned. "You're afraid of dogs, Tess?"

Wrong word, he thought. For terror, once again, was etched into every line of her body, her eyes saturated with emotions he couldn't begin to name, let alone understand.

"I—yes, I'm afraid of them," she faltered. Flushing, she dropped her hold on his suit jacket.

"They thought I was Del."

"I don't care what they thought—just keep them away from me."

"You get bitten as a kid?" he said casually, signaling for the dogs to stay as he led her up the magnificent curve of the stairwell.

"Yes. Yes, I was."

Accusing her of lying would start another argument, Cade decided. But she was definitely lying. Again. He opened the fourth door along the hallway. "The Rose Room," he said ironically. "My mother was, in many ways, very conservative."

An ornate brass bed, too much ruffled chintz, an acre of rose-pink carpet, and a bouquet of real roses on the mantel. "My whole house would fit in here," Tess said.

Cade opened a drawer in the Chippendale dresser and pulled out a nightgown. "Towels and toothbrush in the bathroom," he said brusquely. "Come down for breakfast in the morning any time you're ready."

The gown was a slither of green silk that had probably cost more than her entire wardrobe. As Tess gingerly took it from him, a spark of electricity leaped between them. She jumped back, giving a nervous laugh, tossing the gown on the bed. As though he couldn't help himself, Cade took her by the shoulders. "All too appropriate," he said tightly.

His fingers scorched through her dress; his eyes skewered her to the wall. She tried to twist free. "Don't!"

"You're so goddamn beautiful—I can't keep my hands off you."

Deep within, feelings she'd never experienced before uncoiled in her belly, slowly, lazily, unarguably. Her knees felt weak. Her heart was juddering in her breast. With all her strength, she pushed against the hard planes of Cade's chest.

"If you brought me here to seduce me, you've got the wrong woman. Let go, Cade! *Please...*"

She wasn't a woman who would beg easily. She wasn't playing hard to get, either—he was almost sure of that. Plain and simple, she hated being touched. By him? Or by anyone?

His usual women were willing. All too willing, tediously and predictably so; which was probably why it had been a considerable while since he'd shared his bed.

Cade released her, rubbing his palms down his trousers, and stated the obvious. "You feel the attraction, too. But for some reason you're fighting it."

"I don't feel anything! Or is your ego so inflated you can't stand rejection?"

The wildcat was back, eyes glittering. "You do feel it, Tess. I can read the signals." He gave her a mock salute. "We'll pick this up in the morning. Good night."

The door closed softly behind him. Tess locked it with a decisive snap, then sank down on the bed. She'd never in her life met anyone like Cade Lorimer.

A few moments ago, desire had almost overwhelmed her. Desire was a phenomenon she'd read about, always with faint derision; it wasn't something she'd ever expected to attack her like an enemy from within.

When Tess woke the next morning, the sound of the sea was drowned by the hard pelt of rain driven against the windowpanes.

Trying to shake off a strange sense of oppression, she sat up, and saw with a jolt of unease that an envelope had been pushed under her door.

Opening it as warily as if it contained a deadly virus, Tess unfolded the sheet of heavy vellum. *I'll stay at the hospital all day*, it said. *The housekeeper will find some-*

thing for you to wear and the dogs will be kept in the kennels. Cade.

His handwriting was angular, decisive and very masculine. Cautiously Tess unlocked the door, peeked down the empty hallway and grabbed the small heap of clothes on the floor. Tights, a scoop-necked T-shirt and a pair of sandals that looked brand-new: the housekeeper had come through.

Quickly she dressed and went downstairs for breakfast. She spent the rest of the day curled up in the library, reading and listening to the rain, birch logs snapping in the fireplace. But to her intense annoyance, from midafternoon onward, she found herself straining for the sound of Cade's car.

She wanted him to drive her home. That was the only reason she was interested in his return.

She got up, pacing back and forth, wishing the rain would let up so she could go outdoors. Then, from the corner of her eye, she noticed a collection of framed diplomas on the wall of the alcove beyond the fireplace. Walking closer, she saw degrees from Harvard, awards from the London School of Economics, the letters dancing in front of her eyes.

All the diplomas were Cade's.

Humiliation wasn't an emotion new to Tess; but she'd never before felt it so keenly or so painfully. She hadn't even graduated from high school.

Worse, she was the daughter of a small-time crook and his unscrupulous mistress.

Cade Lorimer was way out of her league. One thing was certain—she'd never be *his* mistress. Not that she wanted to be, of course.

Viciously Tess dug the poker into the glowing coals, tossed another log on the fire and went back to her book.

Dinner was a welcome break, even though her appetite had deserted her. But when Cade still wasn't back by nine o'clock that evening, Tess clumped downstairs to the kitchen. She was trapped in this horrible house for another night, she thought irritably, making herself a mug of hot chocolate, stirring in too many marshmallows, then taking an experimental sip.

Behind her, the swing door swished open. Cade said, "You've got marshmallow on your chin."

She glowered at him. "Nice to see you, too."

"I need a drink—something stronger than hot chocolate."

"How's Del?" she countered; and realized to her surprise that she really wanted to know.

"Cranky as a bear in a cage. Coming home late tomorrow afternoon. Whose clothes are you wearing?"

"The butler's granddaughter's," she said.

The tights were too short and the T-shirt too small. Trying very hard to keep his gaze above the level of her breasts—which were exquisitely shaped—Cade opened the door of the refrigerator, took out a beer and uncapped it. Taking a long draught, he said, "Hospital food has to be the worst in the nation and their tap water tastes like pure chlorine."

He'd dropped onto a stool by the counter and was loosening the collar of his shirt. He looked tired, she thought reluctantly, watching the muscles in his throat move as he swallowed.

His body hair was a dark tangle at the neckline of his shirt; the thin cotton clung to the breadth of his shoulders. As he rolled up his sleeves, corded muscles moved smoothly under his skin. Moved erotically, Tess thought, and buried her nose in her mug. What was wrong with her? She never noticed the way a man moved.

The silence had stretched on too long. She said politely, "Is it still raining?"

"Supposed to stop tomorrow morning." He took another gulp of beer. "What did you do all day?"

"Read in the library."

"Right up your alley," he said with a faint smile.

One smile. That was all. No reason for her to feel as though he'd given her the sun, the moon and the stars. The man had charm to burn, she thought crossly; but she'd always considered charm a slippery attribute at best. Picking up her mug to drain the last of the hot chocolate from it, she said tautly, "If you're not able to drive me home tomorrow morning, I'm sure there's a chauffeur hidden away in this barn of a house. I'll get him to drive me...good night."

"Wait a minute!"

Furious, she glanced down. His fingers—those elegant fingers—were clamped around her left wrist. "Let go," she flared. "I'm not in the mood for macho."

"Del won't be home until the afternoon, and he wants to meet you—so you can't go back before that. And when you meet him, don't say or do anything to upset him. He's to be kept quiet for the next while, and he's not supposed to worry about anything."

"You told him I was here? That I'd meet him?" she said, her voice rising.

"Of course I did. Why else are you here?"

"How was I supposed to leave? I don't have a car, there's no bus to Malagash Island and I don't like hitchhiking in a downpour."

Cade stood up, still clasping her wrist. "You'll meet him, Tess. You don't have to throw your arms around him. But, by God, you'll be polite."

"Is this your CEO act?" she snapped. "Well, whoop-de-doo." Her eyes were like green fire. Not stopping to think, Cade dropped his head and kissed her, hard and fast and with all the pent-up emotion of the last two days. Then he stepped back, his heart juddering in his chest. "I've been wanting to do that ever since I saw you jogging on the beach," he snarled. "You be around when Del comes home, and watch what you say. If you're half the person the islanders say you are, you wouldn't want an old man's death on your conscience."

His kiss, so unexpected, so forceful, had seared through her like a bolt of lightning. Her adrenaline sky-high, any caution lost in rage, Tess wrenched her wrist free and blazed, "You're the one who brought me here—what about *your* conscience?"

"My conscience is my concern. Just behave yourself tomorrow."

"Don't tell me how to behave—I'm twenty-two, not ten," Tess retorted, itching to throw her empty mug in his face. Banging it on the counter instead, she pivoted to leave the room.

Like a steel clamp, Cade's hand closed around her shoulder. "I'm not only telling you how to behave, I expect to be obeyed. Have you got that straight?"

"I'm not an employee you can fire when the whim takes you!"

"No," he said in a voice like ice, "you're Del's grand-daughter." Then, with a deliberation that was subtly insulting, he released her and stepped back.

Was she really related to the old man she'd seen in the hospital? Or was this whole setup as unreliable as a bad dream? Unable to think of a thing to say, as furious with herself as she was with Cade, Tess marched out of the room with as much dignity as she could muster. As she raced up the back stairs, she realized she was scrubbing at her mouth, doing her best to erase a kiss that had been shattering in its heat, its anger and its imperious demands.

No wonder words had deserted her. No wonder she was on the run.

Once again, she locked her bedroom door.

CHAPTER FOUR

BY THE time the rain stopped the next day, an hour after lunch, Tess was in a foul mood. She'd go mad if she didn't get some exercise.

She'd always hated being confined.

While Moorings must be worth a mint, she wouldn't trade it for her cabin for all the money in the world. But would Cade believe her if she told him that? Somehow, she doubted it.

She slipped out the front door. The air was filled with the heady scent of wet pine needles mingled with salt from the sea. Breathing deep, she set off down a narrow path that, she hoped, would lead her to the ocean.

The path ended at a secluded cove ringed by rocks, where the water sparkled and danced, riffling onto a pale sand beach. Quickly she shucked off her borrowed sandals, and dipped her toe in. Cold, yes, but not unbearably so. She looked around. No one in sight, and Cade wouldn't be back until late afternoon.

Like the mischievous little girl she'd never been allowed to be, Tess stripped to her underwear and, giggling breathlessly, ran into the water. In a mighty splash she flopped forward and thrashed toward the rocks.

She'd learned to swim at a local pool the year she'd spent

in Boston as a housekeeper; her strokes were strong, if not particularly stylish. The exercise warmed her, and all the kinks—physical and emotional—of the last forty-eight hours washed away.

Heaven, she thought, turning on her back and floating so she could gaze into the guileless blue sky.

Cade settled Del in the master suite at Moorings, promising to bring Tess to meet him in an hour or so. He then went in search of her.

He drew a blank in the library, the dining room, the solarium and her bedroom. Her black dress was still hanging in the closet; so she couldn't have left.

The beach, he thought. That's where she'd go. Unless she'd left Moorings altogether: she hadn't liked his ultimatum or his CEO act, and he wouldn't put it past her to start walking the highway toward Malagash Island. He hoped to God she wouldn't hitchhike; even on the back roads of Maine, that wasn't a good idea.

If she wasn't at the shore, where would he look next?

He hurried to his room, changed into running gear, and took off down the path. Wet leaves brushed his bare arms, and it was unseasonably warm. He was sweating by the time he emerged onto the beach.

A little heap of clothes lay on the sand and the beach was deserted. Cade jolted to a stop and scanned the surf, his pulse pounding in his ears.

Where the hell was she?

Then he caught sight of a wet head, sleek as a seal's, out by the rocks. Tess. She was cavorting in the waves, diving, splashing and kicking. His relief was instantly engulfed in anger.

He yelled her name. Her head swiveled. She waved at him,

and even from that distance he could see she was laughing. Anger notched up to sheer fury.

He ran the length of the beach, his sneakers sinking into the sand. Then, with ferocious speed, he leaped from rock to rock along the long outcrop of granite. When he was level with her, he shouted, "Come closer—I'll lift you out."

Treading water, she gazed dubiously at the chunks of rock. "I'll swim back to the beach and meet you there."

"Do as you're told. Or so help me, I'll jump in and haul you out."

A wave sloshed over her bare shoulders. Laughing with delight, she said pertly, "It's a gorgeous day! Why are you so angry?"

"Because you could have easily drowned in the undertow—why do you think I'm angry?"

Tess's mouth dropped open. What a ridiculous time to realize that while she'd always been petrified of Cory's rages, Cade's anger didn't frighten her at all. It challenged her instead, invigorating her. And what did that mean?

As another wave slopped up her chin, she swallowed a mouthful of saltwater. Choking and sputtering, her brain grappling with this latest twist, she edged toward the rock and waited for a gap in the surf. Then she reached up for Cade's outstretched hands.

With insulting ease, he lifted her from the water. She found her footing on the rough granite and shook her head like a dog. "You should have come in," she said wickedly, "the water's great."

She was wearing nothing but a skimpy black bra and black bikini underwear. Her image burned into Cade's brain: the thrust of her breasts; her waist's delicate concavity; the flare of hip. Like a peregrine plummeting to its prey, he took her in his arms and found her mouth. Her lips were cold and wet, tasting of salt; as he drank deep, he wasn't so angry that he didn't sense the sudden rigidity of her body and her total lack of response.

From somewhere deep within, he dredged up the will-power to restrain his kiss, seeking rather than demanding, giving rather than taking; and was rewarded when he felt her hands creep up his chest and her body grow pliant. Her first shy response rocketed his heartbeat. He fought for control, nibbling on her lower lip, his tongue seeking out the heated warmth of her mouth.

With the same trust, the same hesitancy, she opened to him.

God, how he wanted her!

He pulled her slender frame the length of his, the fit perfect, the cold nubs of her breasts through her bra further inflaming him. Her hands crept around his neck, her fingers digging into his scalp; the tentative touch of her tongue ripped through him. Fiercely he traced the long curve of her spine, then circled her naked hips, drawing her into the hardness of his arousal.

Tess shuddered, fear ripping through her, banishing an exploration that had totally beguiled her. She pulled her mouth free, and had neither the will nor the strength to mask the turmoil of emotion that was tearing her apart.

Cade said urgently, "Don't be frightened—yes, I want you, no disguising that. But I won't hurt you, I swear I won't."

She was shivering, for the lovely liquid heat of Cade's embrace had vanished. He'd taken her somewhere she'd never been, she thought numbly, and in so doing, had changed her unalterably.

She whispered, "I'm cold. I need to go back to the house."

"Tess, you wanted me as much I wanted you."

She could scarcely deny it. Fighting for control, she

said, "If I'm to meet Del this afternoon, there's a condition attached—you mustn't touch me again. Or kiss me. Do you promise?"

"No."

Her lashes flickered. They were wet, he noticed, stuck together in little clumps. He said, "The only promise I'm prepared to make is that I'll never do anything against your will."

"That's downright manipulative!"

"Is it? Think about it."

She was chewing on her bottom lip. The slope of her shoulders, the delicate flare of her collarbone, juddered through him. "We'd better go back," he said curtly. "Didn't anyone ever tell you not to swim alone? This is the ocean, not some suburban swimming pool."

"I couldn't stand being caged up in that house for one minute longer!"

"You were a fool to take such a risk," he said in a clipped voice. Bending, he gathered her in his arms.

Tess gave a gasp of dismay. One moment she'd been standing on her own two feet; and now she was cheek to chest with the man who was undermining her whole sense of identity. She said in a smothered voice, "Put me down."

But Cade had started back toward the beach, treading carefully over the heaped boulders. "The granite's rough and your feet are bare."

Not up for discussion: that's what he meant. His arm beneath her bare thigh was hard as rock; against her rib cage she could feel the strong, steady beat of his heart, an astonishing intimacy that streaked through her veins like wildfire. How could she feel so threatened by him, yet, paradoxically, so safe?

She closed her eyes, biting her lip to keep the question unspoken. When they reached the beach, Cade dumped her unceremoniously on the sand beside her clothes. "Put them on—I'll find you something dry when we get to the house."

Yanking the tights up her wet legs, she said peevishly, "You weren't supposed to get home until later."

He gave a mirthless smile. "The hospital couldn't wait to get rid of Del. He's home resting. We'll visit him once you're cleaned up."

"I'm not going to meet him wearing a T-shirt that's two sizes too small!"

"Guess it'll have to be the little black dress then." Cade grinned with an aggressive flash of white teeth. "Or one of my T-shirts, which will be four sizes too big."

She tugged her borrowed shirt over her head, noticing with dismay how her nipples were faithfully outlined under the thin fabric. With a sigh of exasperation, she shoved her toes into her sandals. Meeting her alleged grandfather couldn't be nearly as challenging as keeping one step ahead of Cade Lorimer.

An hour later, Tess was ready. She was overdressed, she thought, and decided to do without earrings and to leave her hair loose around her face. Her sweater draped over her black dress, she went in search of Cade; and found him waiting for her in the solarium. It was the only room in the house in which she felt even slightly at home, with its massed ferns and semitropical plants.

Cade swept her from head to toe in a single comprehensive glance. She was nervous, he thought, and doing her best to hide it. "Let's get this over with," he said.

She tossed her head. "I'm not scared of Del Lorimer."

"Good," Cade said blandly. He tucked her arm in his; her fingers were as cold as when he'd pulled her from the ocean. His jaw tight, unable to think of anything to say, he led her out of the room.

Upstairs, he tapped on Del's door. "Come in," Del growled.

His hand at the small of her back, Cade pushed Tess ahead of him.

Del Lorimer was sitting up in a vast iron bed, the sunlight full on his face. Tess stopped dead in her tracks, making a tiny, shocked sound.

His eyes were the same true, deep green as hers.

He really was her grandfather. He had to be. Only now did she realize that, deep down, she'd never fully believed Cade's story.

Del, she noticed, looked every bit as shocked as she felt. He said gruffly, "So you inherited the Lorimer eyes. They skipped Cory. As did so much else." He patted the white bedspread. "Come closer, girl. Let me look at you."

Like a robot, she walked nearer to the bed, and watched him devour every detail of her appearance with those vivid green eyes. He said brusquely, "Let's get the apology out of the way first. I'm sorry the money I sent never reached you. I should have known Cory would take it. But Opal—guess I expected better of her."

Tess blinked. "Apology accepted."

"I owe you, girl. I'm—"

"My name's Tess," she said.

"So you've got claws. Good. Never did like females to be doormats for a feller to wipe his feet on." Del cleared his throat. "Like I said, I owe you. You'll live here in the summers, and in Manhattan in my penthouse the rest of the year. I'll arrange for a monthly allowance starting tomorrow. You can travel, go to college, do what you like. And when I pop off, which at this rate could be any day, you'll inherit a big whack of money."

Battling a mixture of outrage and amusement, Tess said,

"I don't think you're going to pop off—you wouldn't be able to call the shots if you did."

He gave a surprised bark of laughter. "Can't call 'em with Cade. Learned that a long time ago. Might as well try my hand with you."

"What if I'm as contrary as Cade?"

"All that money? Don't make me laugh."

"Surely I'm the one who should be laughing—all the way to the bank."

"I owe you," he repeated stubbornly.

"You don't owe me anything!"

From behind, Cade kicked her ankle with the toe of his shoe. *Behave yourself...* Tess said coolly, "I'll think about everything you've said, Mr. Lorimer—it's a very generous offer. By the way, your beach is beautiful."

"Not bad. Get whales offshore all summer. You can go back to Malagash later today, quit your job, pack your stuff and move up here. I usually head for the city mid-October."

Stubborn, Del most certainly was. But underneath the bluster the old man was exhausted, Tess realized with a pang of compassion. Not that he'd ever admit it. Hadn't she inherited the same will to survive, the same stiff-necked pride? Without them, she might have gone under, years ago.

Impulsively she leaned forward and kissed him on the cheek. "I'm glad we've met...I'll talk to you later." Then, without looking at Cade, she walked out of the room.

Moments later, Cade joined her, closing the door quietly behind him. "We'll go back to the solarium," he said.

It was as good a place as any. When they reached it, Tess stationed herself against a magnificent hibiscus in full bloom, and said with a calmness she was far from feeling, "I understand now why you reacted to the color of my eyes."

"No DNA tests required," he said dryly.

"None are needed anyway—I'm turning down Del's offer." As Cade's breath escaped in an angry hiss, she said passionately, "Hear me out, Cade. And do your best to see where I'm coming from."

He jammed his hands in his pockets. "Okay, give—I'm listening."

She paused, trying to marshal her thoughts. "First, I don't need a grandfather who would serve as a constant reminder of my father. I told you I disliked Cory. The truth is, I loathed him—he never loved me, never saw me as anything but an impediment, an inconvenience."

Cade said intuitively, "You were afraid of him."

"Maybe I was," she said in a brittle voice. "But that's not your concern."

"Why were you afraid of him?"

Ignoring a question she had no intention of answering, she said evenly, "As for Del's money, it would stifle me. I'm financially independent, in debt to no one, with a job I like and my own place to live. I'm not giving that up to move to this house—it's too formal, and I hate tripping over servants all the time. It'd be like living in a velvet-upholstered cage!"

"You want control over your own life."

"Why wouldn't I?"

"Why not try compromise instead of control? You're not giving Del a chance."

"It's my life. He might feel he owes me—but I don't owe him anything. Can't you understand? He's nothing to me. Nothing!"

"Who are you trying to convince—yourself?"

"You! But you aren't listening."

Cade's eyes narrowed. "My problem is, I'm listening to

both of you—you and Del. Let me tell you something. I own a house a couple of miles down the road, and you can stay there in the summers, use the place as if it's your own—I'm often away. You'd be close enough to Del, yet preserve your independence."

"What's the point? I'd only be substituting one cage for another."

"My house is very different from Moorings. Modern, full of light and open to the ocean—you'd like it, I know you would. It's my favorite, I have to admit."

"Favorite? You own other houses?"

"Sure—a brownstone in Manhattan. A château on the Loire, a lodge at the vineyard in South Australia."

The question was out before she could censor it. "Just how rich are you, Cade?"

He named a number and watched her jaw drop. "I was a computer whiz kid," he said. "Made a bundle early, invested it, and haven't stopped since. I took over Lorimer Inc. from Del seven years ago, when he turned sixty-five, and I've expanded it considerably." His smile was sardonic. "Your inheritance from Del won't come near my net worth, but it'll be sizable just the same."

Tess gave a sudden shiver. "I hate it when you talk that way."

"Do you? Do you really?"

She walked over to the window without answering him, staring out at the formal gardens, her fingers pleating and re-pleating the black fabric of her skirt. Cade followed her, his gaze fastened on her face. She was thinking, he decided, and thinking hard. Which was, of course, an all too natural reaction. Money—the amount he'd mentioned—would give a saint cause to think; and Tess, being a woman, was by definition no saint. Besides, she was dirt poor.

So what if he was a cynic? He'd had plenty of cause to become one in the last several years.

Tess said so quietly Cade had to strain to hear her, "Why did you tell me how rich you are?"

"You did ask. And isn't it better to get it out in the open?"

"So much money…" she breathed, resting her forehead on the glass pane and closing her eyes.

So she'd succumbed, Cade thought. And why not? Money was an extraordinarily potent weapon. Money, in the circles in which he moved, was the equivalent to power.

He should know.

He raked his fingers through his hair. Disconcertingly a big part of him wished Tess had held out. That she was different from all the other women he'd met.

How silly was that?

CHAPTER FIVE

SLOWLY Tess straightened, turning around to face Cade, the leaves of the hibiscus brushing her arm. End this whole charade now, she thought, before it's too late. She opened her mouth to speak, with no idea how she was going to end anything.

The late sun was firing her hair with gold. Cade said, moving smoothly into the next phase of his strategy, "As the Lorimer heiress, there are things you'll need to know—we have a lot of ground to cover. We'll start by touring the headquarters of Lorimer Inc. in Manhattan, then move to its international holdings. It'd be best to visit them one by one. Nothing like seeing a setup in person, and talking with the employees, to get a grasp on the way things operate."

Her face pale, Tess pushed away from the window ledge. "Are you crazy?" she croaked. "I'm not—"

"No wealth without social responsibility and intelligent understanding—that's Del's credo, and it's one I endorse," he said. "The château on the Loire that I mentioned, we'll go there after New York. Then we'll stay in the DelMer hotel in Venice—that'll show you another part of the operation. After that, there's the thoroughbred farm in Kentucky, our oil holdings in Venezuela, and the vineyards near Adelaide."

She was gaping at him, temporarily speechless. Good thing

she couldn't read his mind, Cade thought. The prospect of traveling around the world with her—necessary though it was—appalled him. How was he going to keep his hands off her? Or get a decent night's sleep, knowing she was on the other side of the wall?

Seducing Tess Ritchie wasn't part of his strategy; it would be neither responsible nor intelligent.

"You have to be educated to your new position," he went on. "It's important you take your rightful place in Del's world, and be comfortable in it. Afterward, you can be as proactive in Lorimer Inc. as you wish. This plan, by the way, has Del's blessing."

"You talked it over with him?" Tess said with the calm of extreme rage.

"Of course. At the hospital today while we were waiting for him to be discharged."

Cade stepped closer, tweaking a strand of her hair. "I guess the first step—rather than Manhattan—should be a proper haircut and some decent clothes." Of its own volition, his hand strayed to her cheek, stroking the silken sweep of her skin, lingering there. His loins tightened.

She struck his hand away. "I'm not going to Manhattan. Or Venice. I'm not going anywhere with you."

"The haircut and the clothes—enough clothes to start with, anyway—we can deal with those in Camberley."

Camberley was a nearby shopping area patronized by the very rich. "If I'm not going with you, I don't need to go to Camberley," Tess seethed. "I have a job waiting for me—they're expecting me to show up tomorrow morning at nine. If you won't drive me back to Malagash, I'll call a cab and go on my own."

"Your job isn't waiting for you—I phoned yesterday and arranged for an extended leave of absence."

"You *phoned* them? Behind my back, without even telling me?"

"There was no point in telling you—you'd have raised the roof."

Cade was standing between her and the door. Tess put a hand to his chest, pushing him as hard as she could; and was further infuriated when he didn't move an inch. "Where's the nearest telephone?" she demanded. "It'll be the shortest leave of absence on record."

He dropped his hands to her shoulders, his nails digging into her skin. "Stop being so childish."

Her eyes like green pools of fire, she spat, "You think you can *buy* me? Wave a million dollars in front of me and I'll meekly fall into line? Some things can't be bought, Cade Lorimer, and my freedom is one of them. Now get out of my way!"

"I never thought you were a coward," he said.

"Coward?" she repeated incredulously. "Because I'm not genuflecting to you and your precious money?"

"Because you're turning your back on the chance to make something of yourself," he retorted, his voice like a whiplash. "You've got a two-bit job on an insignificant island and you live in a fish shack. Is that what you want for the rest of your life?"

"I'm twenty-two, Cade. Not sixty."

"You're turning your back on world travel. On gaining insider information about one of the largest international corporations in existence. On the opportunity to further your education anywhere and in any field you want. Yeah, you're a coward. A coward and a fool."

White-faced with rage, she seethed, "I'm neither one. I'm a survivor who's lived in places you've never dreamed of. I don't need you, your money or your fancy international connections. Or your ivory tower existence—what do *you* know about the real world? You're totally insulated from it!"

He knew a great deal about the real world, knowledge that had been hard earned. Not that he was going to tell her that. Some things he'd learned long ago to keep to himself.

Cutting to the chase with the speed of a predator, he said, "You never went to university—am I right?"

Her shoulders slumped. "You have a genius for finding my weak points," she said with the honesty of despair. "I've never even finished high school—the only reason I got the job at the Malagash library was that they were desperate."

"You'd like more education, wouldn't you?"

"Of course. But I have my living to earn."

"No, you don't—Del's giving you an allowance. That's the whole point."

"A kept woman," she said bitterly.

"Stop wallowing in clichés, you're far too intelligent for that. Fact number one—you're Del's granddaughter. Fact number two—he's a very rich man who wants to make amends for the past. Fact number three—his health's not great and he mustn't be stressed. It wouldn't hurt you to go along with him for now and it sure as hell could benefit you."

He made it sound so easy, so logical. Yet panic was engulfing Tess at the mere thought of leaving the life she'd carefully and painstakingly fashioned for herself. "I don't want to leave the island," she cried. "I'm afraid to."

There. She'd said it.

"I know you are—that's where the courage comes in," Cade said straightforwardly; and somehow, in the midst of it all, she noticed with a twinge of respect that he wasn't offering her empty sympathy. "We'll start small," he added. "The haircut and the clothes first, then we'll go from there. One step at a time."

She said slowly, "What's in this for you?"

An opportunity to test my willpower, he thought crazily. To practice celibacy in the company of a woman who drives me—and my hormones—up the wall. "I'm doing it for Del," he said, and knew he was skirting the borders of truth.

Tess wrapped her arms around her chest. "Why does everything have to be so complicated?"

"Because simplicity's boring?"

"You're not boring."

"Neither are you," Cade said with such vehemence that Tess's mouth twitched in an involuntary smile.

She said, "By the time you've finished shepherding me around the world, you'll be bored out of your skull."

"I wouldn't count on it," he said grimly, brought her hand to his lips and kissed her palm with a sensual pleasure that melted every bone in her body.

Hot color flooded her cheeks. She snatched her hand back. "When you act like that, I want to run in the opposite direction!"

"You can't—it's too late to run away."

He was right, although she couldn't have said at what point it had become too late. "So I'm cornered," she retorted, biting off her words. "Del mustn't be upset or worried—guess I can't march into his room and tell him I'm heading back to Malagash on the first ferry, can I? You've manipulated me from the very beginning, Cade. Congratulations."

"We'll go shopping tomorrow," he said evenly, "then head for Manhattan the day after. In the meantime, I have work to do in my office here. See you later."

The door to the solarium closed behind him. Tess sat down hard in the nearest chair and kicked off her shoes. Camberley, Manhattan, France and Venice. With Cade.

The die was cast. And her predominant emotion was—heaven help her—excitement.

Swathed in a purple cape, Tess gazed at herself in the mirror. Pierre, the stylist, lifted one long strand of her hair and scrutinized the ends. With a theatrical shudder he demanded, "Who cut your hair?"

"I did," she said. "With the kitchen scissors."

He struck his forehead with the back of his hand. "What brand of conditioner?"

Her budget hadn't included such luxuries. "None."

"*Madame*," he said, "you have come to the right place and only just in time. We will get to work." He bundled her hair back from her face, pulling it this way and that. "Yes. I see the way to go." Imperiously he waved to one of his acolytes. "Shampoo and a treatment first."

An hour and a half later, Tess was again gazing at her reflection. "That's me?" she croaked.

"It is my creation," Pierre said grandly. "You will come back in six weeks, not one day longer."

But Tess wasn't listening. Pierre had cut off great chunks of her hair so that it now framed her face in soft curls. Experimentally she tossed her head, feeling light and somehow free, all the weight gone.

Without any false vanity, she knew she also looked astoundingly beautiful, as though her features had come into their own. Perhaps, she thought slowly, she'd been hiding behind her mass of curls for years, using them as camouflage, as protection; and now she was standing in the open. Exposed.

Cade had accused her of cowardice. She tilted her chin, daring her own reflection. "I—thank you, Pierre," she said inadequately.

Pierre gave a satisfied smile. "You were a challenge—*mon plaisir, madame*."

Cade was waiting for her outside, Tess remembered. Cade, who from the beginning had found her beautiful. Feeling absurdly shy, Tess walked out into the autumn sunshine.

Cade had browsed the local bookstore, and was leaning against the Maserati, trying to keep his attention on the book he had bought. He couldn't. His mind persisted in wandering, and everywhere it went it came up against a chestnut-haired woman with a mind of her own.

Either Tess Ritchie was a brilliant actor, or she really didn't want Del's money. Del's or his.

Considering the amount of time he and Tess had spent together, he knew very little about her. Acting could well be one of her major talents.

Could he trust her? Hadn't he be burned too many times by women who'd wanted him solely for himself—so they'd claimed—only to demand financial recompense when he'd ended the affair? Not one of them had been able to separate him from his money, or to value him for himself.

Poor little rich guy, he thought ironically. Self-pity had never, in his opinion, been an admirable trait. But—just once—he'd like to be seen as a man, not as a walking bank account.

Then something caused him to look up.

Tess was coming down the salon steps toward him. His heartbeat stuttered in his chest. He pushed away from the car, watching her until she was standing only five feet from him. Bravado masking shyness, he thought, and shoved down a totally unwanted flick of respect. "I've already told you you're beautiful," he said flatly. "So now what do I say?"

She blushed. "If I ever cut my hair again with the kitchen

scissors, Pierre will hunt me down. Mercilessly. I was a challenge, or so he said."

"He and I are in total agreement. You are, very definitely, a challenge."

"The head of Lorimer Inc. challenged by a woman who lives in a fish shack?" she said incredulously. "It's the other way around, Cade."

"Is it? Why?"

She scowled at him. "Clothes are the next step in your plan," she said, "not interrogation."

She was right, of course. He wasn't interested in the way her mind worked. It was her body that was obsessing him, not her mind.

"The boutique's one block down the street," he said, and mockingly crooked his elbow. "Shall we go?"

With the sense she was doing something of enormous consequence, Tess rested her hand on his arm. She said provocatively, adjusting her stride to his, "If you pay for my clothes, it'll be all over town that I'm your mistress—or don't you care?"

"I've let it be known that Del's granddaughter, who's been living in Europe, is here for a visit—I prefer gossip to be at least minimally accurate." He glanced down at her. "Would you like to be my mistress?"

"No!"

"Probably just as well, seeing as I haven't asked you."

She dropped his arm as if it was scalding her, the rose-bushes that lined the entrance to the boutique brushing against her legs. "How will I know what to buy here?" she demanded.

"I've spoken to Susan, the owner—she'll see that you have everything you need."

"You're not coming in with me!"

Cade had learned a long time ago that on occasion it was

strategic to be seen to retreat; he owed the boardrooms of Europe a debt of gratitude, he thought wryly. "I'll be waiting near the car," he said.

Tess watched him walk away, letting out her breath in a small hiss. She'd been primed for a fight, and he'd denied her the satisfaction. He moved, she thought unwillingly, with the grace and economy of an athlete; he had the shoulders of an athlete, too.

Furious with herself, she pushed open the door of the boutique. A bell chimed; an attractive, middle-aged woman said, "Can I help you?" Her eyes widened. "You must be Tess Ritchie," she said with genuine warmth, "I've been looking forward to meeting you. Selena—Cade's mother—was a good friend of mine, such a lovely woman."

With a swift glance Tess ascertained they were alone in the boutique. She said, "My hose are from the dollar store, my shoes are secondhand and my dress is homemade. Tomorrow Cade and I are going to New York, then on to France, Venice and heaven knows where. I need help. Major help."

Susan laughed. "You've come to the right place." She marched over to the door, switched the Open sign to Closed and drew the gauze curtain. "Let's have some fun."

Linen, leather, fine wool, silk. Slacks, bras, shoes, earrings. Casual, semiformal, elegant. And always, in the mirror, a woman who was a stranger to Tess: a woman who bore little resemblance to a small-town librarian on a coastal island.

At the end, when Susan was adding up the bill, Tess said, "I'll be paying the first $900." She knew to a penny the amount in her savings account; she was leaving enough money to fly back from Adelaide should she need to.

Susan's fingers paused on the till. "Cade didn't mention you paying for anything," she said dubiously.

"Cade Lorimer is much too used to getting his own way." Tess held out her credit card. "The first $900."

"He's in for a shock with you."

"It'll be good for him."

Tess signed the receipt and gave Susan a quick hug. "Thank you so much. You've been a lifesaver."

"My pleasure," Susan said, uncannily echoing Pierre. "I'll see that everything's delivered to Moorings later today. Have fun on your travels, Tess—I mean that."

"I'll do my best," Tess said, smiling, and walked outside into the sunshine.

Her pumps were Italian leather, her hose silk. Her underwear was also silk, edged with the finest of lace. Her suit, with its cheeky little flared skirt and neat-fitting jacket, was cerise linen, teamed with a cream silk blouse; her earrings were simple gold hoops. With a new confidence in her step, Tess crossed the road and saw Cade walking down a side street toward her.

She met him partway, flipped her new Chanel dark glasses up into her hair, and passed him the bill. "I cost you plenty," she said. "I really liked Susan, by the way."

He flicked down the bill. "Not as much as I'd expected."

"I paid the first $900," Tess said calmly. "That way I'm only partially a kept woman."

"You can't afford to do that!"

"You let me decide what I can and can't afford," she said softly, and knew she was talking about far more than clothes.

"Sometimes I will," he replied with the same dangerous softness, "and sometimes I won't."

"Then you'll keep me on my toes, won't you?" she said, glancing down at her exquisite new shoes.

"While I was waiting, I arranged our flights to Manhattan and Paris."

"You said one step at a time! That's two steps. Don't push your luck, Cade."

A muscle twitched in his jaw. "You're the most contentious woman I've ever met."

"Flexibility in the face of opposition is a sign of maturity," she remarked airily.

The seawind was gently flipping her skirt, exposing even more of those glorious long-stemmed legs. For wasn't she like a flower, Cade thought, colorful, graceful, burnished with sunlight? *Flowers are for picking,* a voice said in his head.

Not this flower.

So now you're the coward, Cade?

With an incoherent exclamation compounded of frustration, lust and fury, Cade put his arms around Tess, pulled her to his body and plunged for her mouth. In sheer shock, she opened to him. He thrust with his tongue in an assault as unsubtle as it was steeped in raw hunger. More hunger slammed through him, his heart like a piston in his chest, his loins hard with primitive need.

Her scent, her softness shafted his body with lethal speed. He was lost...

He wasn't lost. He was on the main street of Camberley ravishing Del's granddaughter in full daylight. As though someone had thrown cold water in his face, Cade wrenched his head free.

And met a pair of wide-held green eyes, turbulent with emotions he couldn't begin to guess. Patches of color rode high in Tess's cheeks. Her shoulders were rigid in his grip. Cade said choppily, "If I was smart, I'd head for Manhattan on my own on the first plane."

"Go right ahead," she gasped.

"No way—I never back down from a challenge." He gave his wolfish grin. "It would ruin my reputation."

His answer wasn't in any way reassuring. Tess gazed up at him blankly, her breath lodged somewhere in her throat, and her knees on the point of collapse; she was also, she realized distantly, trembling. The desire that had streaked through her veins from Cade's kiss was indeed her enemy, its sole aim to drive her into intimacy with a man who screamed danger from every pore. For if his kiss had been passionate, it had also been passionately angry.

Intimacy? The word was as much a stranger to her as the man. Yet she'd agreed to traipse around four continents with him in the next few weeks.

She was out of her mind.

Her voice thin in her ears, she said, "I can always run away, Cade. And I will, if you push me too far."

"I can always bring you back."

"I'm good at vanishing," she said, "I've had lots of practice. You might want to remember that."

Even now, knowing he'd just made a major mistake in judgment—lust blinding him to any remnant of reason—Cade had to fight the urge to seize her in his arms and kiss her again. He'd never felt so out of control, so at the mercy of a woman's body. Although that's all it was, a body. Dammit, the only thing he was feeling was the basic attraction between male and female. Lust. Chemistry. Testosterone.

Nothing else.

And that's the way it was going to stay.

CHAPTER SIX

SIXTEEN minutes later, Cade pulled the Maserati to a halt outside Moorings. He reached for a leather briefcase in the back seat, opened it and said, "I might as well give you this stuff now, Tess."

He passed her some papers, a checkbook and a credit card. "Everything's been set up in your name. This is the balance in the account, and this amount will be added on the first of every month. Oh, and here's the limit on the credit card."

Tess sat still, gazing at numbers that scarcely seemed real; once again, the ground had shifted under her feet. "That's far too much," she said.

"You'll get used to it," he replied cynically.

"Gee, thanks for the vote of confidence. Who's money is it?"

"Del's—I'm just the messenger."

Just wasn't a word that applied to Cade Lorimer, she thought, drumming her fingers on her knee. "Do you know how I feel?" she said tightly. "As though you're robbing me of everything I cherish—my solitude and independence, my job, my little house, my freedom." She riffled through the blank checks. "And you've got the gall to substitute money in their place...all to prevent an arrogant old man from getting upset."

Are you for real about the money?

Cade looked at her in silence. She gave every impression of speaking from the heart, he thought, and along with the distrust that was his constant companion, felt a flicker of remorse. How long since anyone had caused him to question his motives, or to see firsthand the results of his own actions?

It's for your own good… while this was true enough, maybe she deserved better of him. But his mind remained stubbornly blank of alternatives, the silence stretching in front of him like a sun-baked desert.

In sudden impatience, Tess ran her fingers through her hair. "I don't know why I thought you'd understand—silly of me. When all's said and done, I agreed to this charade, didn't I? Let's go and see Del and get it over with."

"Not until you've calmed down."

She said bitterly, "Don't worry, I'll behave myself. In my fancy clothes and my expensive new shoes."

He pounced. "Why *are* you embarking on this charade, as you call it—what's the real reason?"

Tess bit her lip; he couldn't have asked a more difficult question. "I haven't figured it out yet," she said evasively.

"When you do," he said nastily, "let me know, won't you?"

"Maybe. Maybe not." She tilted her chin. "My reasons might be private."

"I'm sure they are—and with good reason."

"You persist in suspecting me of the worst!"

She was right. He did. With impersonal briskness Cade said, "We'd better go visit Del—he needs to settle down early, and we're leaving first thing in the morning. So this is your only chance to say goodbye to him."

If only she had a weapon—any weapon—that would force Cade to see her as she really was. That would make even a minimal impression on him. But the prospect was laughable;

the mighty Cade Lorimer had a hide as tough as his leather briefcase. Tess preceded him into the house and up the stairs, carrying the sheaf of papers under her arm.

Del's bedroom door was open. The old man was sitting in an armchair that overlooked the blue waters of the cove; although his face was turned away, there was both sadness and frustration in his bearing. Pity sliced through her. He was a widower who'd lost a beloved wife; and during the last few weeks, he'd been exiled from health and vigor.

Tapping on the door to give him a moment to recover, she said lightly, "This is the new me. Do you need an introduction?"

Stiffly Del turned his head; his eyes widened. "You remind me of Selena," he said unevenly. "My second wife. Cade's mother. She was a beauty—stole the breath from my body until the day she died."

More moved than she cared to admit, Tess said softly, "Thank you, Mr. Lorimer. That's a lovely thing to say."

"What do you plan to call me, girl? Because you can drop the Mr. Lorimer crap."

"I'll call you Del if you'll quit calling me girl."

He gave a bark of laughter. "Done deal. So you're off to Manhattan tomorrow."

"Yes," she said. "Although I reserve the right at any time to go home to Malagash Island."

"Cade better make damn sure you don't."

"It may not be up to Cade—I have a mind of my own."

"So does Cade," Del said with a fierce grin.

"Then may the better man—or woman—win," Tess said, tossing her head.

"If you two have finished squaring off like a couple of roosters," Cade said, "I've got work to do."

But Tess wasn't finished. Indicating the sheaf of papers

under her arm, she said awkwardly, "Thank you for this, Del. You've been extremely generous and I promise I won't waste your money."

"Have fun with it," Del said gruffly. "Reckon there hasn't been much fun in your life up to now."

"I will." Quickly Tess stepped closer, kissed his wrinkled cheek and whispered in his ear, "Thanks, Gramps."

His snort of delighted laughter followed her out of the room. Cade was close on her heels. When they were out of earshot of the bedroom, he grated, "You've got him eating out of your hand already—well done, Tess."

She whirled in a flare of skirts. "You don't want him upset—but when I'm nice to him, you don't like that, either. What's your problem?"

For my whole life I've wanted something Del wouldn't give me...yet already he's giving it to you. Cade sure wasn't going to say that. But his brain—his much-vaunted brain—wouldn't come up with anything else. Action. That's what he needed. He grabbed her around the waist, pulled her toward him and kissed her hard on her lips. She kicked out at him. Ignoring the sharp pain in his shin, he deepened the kiss, demanding from her a different response, calling on all his considerable skills to evoke it.

Tess surrendered, suddenly, generously and completely, for what other choice did she have? Her body was melting in his embrace, and of their own accord her arms wound themselves around his neck, her fingers digging into his scalp. It was a kiss she wanted never to end...

Her mouth, that exquisite mouth, melded with Cade's in a way that drove him to the brink. He was steeped in her. Scorched by her. If he didn't have her, he'd explode.

His tongue laced with hers. His hands pushed aside the

lapels of her jacket, finding, under the silken fabric, the warm swell of her breast. Her shudder of response rocketed through him; her nipple had hardened, her body arching into his until there was nothing in the world but this woman, so willing, so achingly desirable.

He was ravishing her not thirty feet from Del's bedroom door.

With a muffled sound of self-disgust, Cade thrust her away. "I don't know what happens to me when I'm around you," he snarled. "My brains go into reverse."

She was trembling, he saw with renewed fury. Her lips were swollen from his kiss, her eyes dazed. "You can't do that to me!" she cried. "Kiss me as though I'm the only woman in the world, then shove me away as if I revolt you."

Nothing could be further from the truth, that much Cade knew. But how much easier it would be if Tess believed he was only toying with her. "I'll do what I want," he said, and watched her quiver as if he'd struck her.

Recoiling, she whispered, "You hate me."

"I hate what you do to me!"

"Yet we're supposed to travel together?"

His own question, precisely: one that had haunted him the last two nights. "You know what the problem is?" he said with deliberate brutality. "I need to find myself a woman. One who knows the score."

Pain tore through her defences. "So you're not really kissing *me*—anyone would do."

"Not just anyone. She has to be beautiful, sophisticated and temporary. Too many stars in your eyes for my liking."

Her nostrils flared; even her hair seemed to spark with electricity. "I'm not afraid of my feelings, if that's what you mean."

"Wearing your heart on your sleeve is plain stupidity."

"Not having one is worse."

"That's—"

"Right now, I wouldn't kiss you if you were the last man in Manhattan. Your whole life's a lie, Cade. Going behind my back with my job, tricking me into protecting Del, manipulating me to suit your own ends. I don't hate you—I despise you!"

So he'd succeeded, Cade thought. She'd avoid him as much as was possible in the next few days; and he, heaven help him, wouldn't lay as much as a finger on her.

To his fury, there was an icy lump lodged in his gut. He said curtly, "Be ready to leave at eight in the morning. I'll have Thomas bring some suitcases to your room."

Then he turned on his heel and marched down the hallway. Lust, that's all it was. Straightforward lust.

Of an intensity and degree beyond his experience.

The next afternoon, Tess was waiting for Cade in the atrium of Lorimer Inc.'s Mahattan headquarters. Steel, glass and light, she thought, gazing upward at the soaring ceiling. Meant to impress, and succeeding brilliantly.

Just as, against her better judgment, Cade had impressed her throughout the day. The empire over which he exercised control was vaster and more complex than she could possibly have imagined; yet every detail was at his fingertips. Furthermore, his employees, from the cleaner on the fourth floor to the vice president on the eighteenth, clearly respected him, responding to him with a warmth he must have earned.

He couldn't have fooled everyone on eighteen floors… could he? Okay, so at work he wasn't just frighteningly intelligent and enormously efficient, he was also a charmer. He'd remembered that the cleaner had a new grandson. He'd inquired with real concern about the vice president's sick wife. He'd listened to a secretary's problem with her medical insurance, and acted on the spot to fix it.

Cory had had charm. He'd turned it on—and off—like the kitchen tap.

So was Cade a classic case of Jekyll and Hyde? After all, she had yet to meet any of his mistresses, the women who consorted with him after working hours. They might have a very different tale to tell than the cleaning lady.

She, Tess, wouldn't be joining their ranks. She was too starry-eyed, too unsophisticated. He was going to hook up with a woman who knew the score.

That would be just fine, Tess thought fiercely. She herself didn't do sex, and she avoided intimacy like the plague. Another woman would get Cade—dangerous Cade—off her back and let her settle into her new role as the Lorimer protégée.

She had no idea what this role would entail. A further loss of freedom? Or an opening to vistas she'd never dared imagine? Either way, the sooner Cade found himself a new mistress, the better.

Then, with a lurch of her heart, she saw him striding across the expanse of marble floor toward her. Dark navy business suit, silk tie, black hair impeccably groomed: if only that were all. Add his height, his breadth of shoulder, the way he moved. Add muscles toned to an animal grace. Add light and shadow falling across the hard planes of his face, across unfathomable gray eyes and features that were infused with strength and character.

The grand total was a magnetism so powerful that every woman from the basement to the penthouse would flock to him.

Including her? Was she fooling herself, big-time?

Gritting her teeth, Tess stood her ground. Cade said with chilling formality, "My chauffeur's outside in the limo, he'll drive you home. We have tickets to the opera tonight—we'll eat before we go, because we have another early start tomorrow and you look tired."

She was. But he didn't have to say so. He didn't look tired, she thought petulantly. He looked like he could work a forty-eight-hour day and go to six operas.

"Oh," he added, "wear a long gown, won't you?"

"Yes, Mr. Lorimer."

His eyes narrowed. "I hoped the tour would have taught you that I value initiative more than compliance."

"Will there be a quiz?" she said naughtily.

"Stow it."

"Do your mistresses turn into paper dolls when you use that tone of voice?" she asked with genuine interest.

"You'll have to ask them. I'll be back before six."

Turning on his heel, he strode toward the elevators. Tess dragged her eyes away, and hurried outside. The chauffeur drove her back to Cade's elegant brownstone near Central Park. She let herself in, ran upstairs to her bedroom, where they'd dropped off her suitcases this morning, and tore off her classy pantsuit. Then she showered in the ultramodern bathroom with its granite counters and heated towel rails, dressed casually in jeans, and laid out on her bed one of the three evening gowns Susan had helped her choose. This one was a deep moss-green, and very becoming. She needed all the help she could get, for wasn't she dreading an outing that would bring her face-to-face with Cade's peers? Or, worse, with the women in his past?

What would it be like to make love to Cade? To surrender herself to him, to be naked in his arms?

With a tiny sound of distress, she tossed the dress on the bed and started prowling the brownstone. Cade liked bold colors, furniture with clean lines and modern art whose impact was visceral. She lingered in front of an array of photographs on the mantel in the living room, in particular one of a much younger Del with his arm around his beautiful, raven-haired Selena. Cade—perhaps nine or ten—was standing on the other side of Del. Del, Tess thought in puzzlement, was making no effort to draw the boy into the photo: all Del's attention and certainly all his feelings were directed toward his new wife.

Already Cade's eyes were full of secrets…

Unexpectedly behind her, with the slightest of sounds, a door swung on its hinges. Tess grabbed a soapstone sculpture from the mantel, whirled in a blur of movement and crouched, holding the statue like a weapon in front of her.

Cade was standing in the doorway.

Slowly Tess straightened, wishing the marble hearth would swallow her and the statue, wishing Cade to the eighteenth floor of Lorimer Inc. She said inadequately, "You startled me."

He walked into the room, took the sculpture from her nerveless fingers, replaced it on the mantel, then stepped back; her reaction, so swift, so practiced, had horrified him. "Don't lie to me!"

"I'm—"

"Your reaction when you heard the sound of the door—what kind of upbringing did you have?"

"That's got nothing—"

"Give it up—you were ready in an instant to defend yourself. To the death, by the look on your face. It's time to come clean…I need to know the facts. The places you've lived. Why you were so terrified the first time you met me."

"Give me one good reason why I should tell you anything! You don't like me. You don't even trust me—you think I'm after every cent you've ever made."

Cade gazed at the defiant flags of color in Tess's cheeks, scarcely hearing what she said, making no attempt to close the gap between them. Keep it that way, he told himself. Don't touch her no matter what you do. But damn well make sure you get some answers. "You were afraid of Cory—why? Did he abuse you?"

"I don't owe you an explanation." Tess backed up until the ledge was digging into her shoulders. Until she could retreat no further, she thought frantically, and like a cornered animal, went on the attack. "Why do you always call your father Del, and not Dad?" she demanded, and made a wild guess. "Because he didn't love you as a little boy?"

Cade's jaw tightened; she had a talent for striking where he was most vulnerable. "That's none of your business."

"Not a bad reply. I'll use the same one."

A *worthy opponent*...where had those words come from? "Maybe Del didn't welcome me into the family the way I would have liked," Cade said tautly. "But he gave me a secure childhood, happier than most kids get, and he did his best to send me out into the world prepared for what I'd find. I'd stake every dollar I ever made that you had none of that."

"If you're so interested in my childhood, why don't you hire your own investigator?" she flared. "You can afford to, we both know that."

The truth slapped Cade in the face. He said baldly, "I don't want to. I don't want to go behind your back, or have a complete stranger ferreting out the details of your life. I want you to tell me yourself."

"You want me to *trust* you?" she said with an incredulity that grated on his nerves.

"Anything you tell me will never go beyond this room, and I'll never use it against you."

"Even if that were true, why would I unload on you? I've never told anyone about my parents or my past."

"If you don't tell me, then I *will* hire my own investigator."

"You know what your problem is—you can't bear to lose."

"You got it. So which is it to be, Tess?" He jammed his hands in his pockets. "Confession's good for the soul, isn't that what they say?"

"Psychobabble."

"Wisdom. Either way, give it a try."

She let out her breath in a small sigh and wandered over to the window, with its view of a quiet, tree-lined street: an oasis of peace in a huge city. Keeping his hands in his pockets, Cade followed her, stationing himself where he could watch her face.

He had no idea what he was about to hear. But he did know it was essential he hear it.

Speaking more to herself than to Cade, Tess said, "Cory's casual acquaintances always liked him. He was astonishingly good-looking, with charm to burn. He was also a heroin addict who stole, cheated and lied. As for Opal, she was beautiful, rich, wild and willful, with the morals of an alley cat—they were well-matched. I, of course, was an accident. I put a big crimp in their style until I was old enough to be left alone."

"How old was that?"

"Five. Six. They used to lock me in my room and go out, and I never knew when they'd come home or what shape they'd be in…I used to fantasize about running away. But I had no money and nowhere to go. No relatives, Cory said, no grandparents—of course they never told me about Del and his money."

"Are you suggesting they were model parents until you were five?"

She winced, and with one finger began tracing the molding on the window, up and down, up and down. "We lived in Madrid until I was five," she said tonelessly. "I had a nanny called Ysabel. I adored her. She was a fiery-tempered Spaniard who stood up to my parents, made sure I got proper food and rest, and took me to the park to play with other children…I used to call her Bella because I couldn't get my tongue around Ysabel."

"What happened to her?"

"Two days after my fifth birthday, Cory, Opal and I got on a train late at night and traveled from Madrid to Vienna. I never saw Ysabel again. Even though I cried and cried, my parents wouldn't give me her phone number so I could call up and say goodbye…a couple of weeks later, they told me she'd died."

"It broke your heart."

For the first time, Tess looked full at him. Dry-eyed, he noticed, for all that those eyes were green pools of pain. "I've never loved another human soul since Ysabel," she said. "Love betrays you. Leaves you bereft, and lonelier than you thought possible."

"Not always," he said harshly. "Sure, I grieved when my mother died. But I was the richer because we loved each other."

Once again, Tess realized, Cade had given honesty instead of easy sympathy. She said stonily, "That hasn't been my experience."

"You never called your parents Mum and Dad?"

"They wouldn't answer if I did."

"Not roles they aspired to," Cade said, remembering Del. Del hadn't wanted to be his father. It had taken Cade years to admit that simple, devastating truth.

"*Did* Cory abuse you?" he asked.

"No. Oh, I got slapped around a few times, usually when they were desperate for a fix and out of money. But nothing major."

That last phrase, he thought, revealed a great deal about

the little girl Tess had been: her daily life so frightening that to be slapped around was unimportant. Although he was almost sure he knew the answer, he said, "Why did you leave Madrid?"

"Creditors were after Cory. It set the pattern—stay in a city until it became too risky, then run away in the night and set up somewhere else. Sometimes the money flowed like water, sometimes there was none." She shivered. "No stability. No safety."

"Until you ended up on Malagash."

"You see why I'm a loner, and why I loved my little cabin? It was mine. I was in control. And I was safe."

"You're safe here," Cade said forcefully.

With equal force Tess said, "One thing I've learned over the years is to create my own safety."

"You can ask others for help."

"You, you mean?" she said with another incredulous laugh. "I don't think so."

Why was he so angry, when, basically, she was telling him what he wanted to hear? He'd never gone out of his way for any of his mistresses; to have done so would have been counter to the whole way he ran his life.

Yet Tess had trusted him with her narrative; and it had had the ring of truth. Or rather, he thought, she'd partially trusted him; for he was aware of the gaps in her story, gaps that left plenty for the imagination. The year she'd turned sixteen, for instance, was still a blank, as were all the years after that.

Later. Bide your time, Cade, choose when to push deeper. In the next few days, there'll be plenty of opportunities.

He would push. He knew he would. Even if he didn't fully understand why.

"We should eat, Tess," he said. "Then we have to get ready—the opera starts at eight."

She was twisting her hands together. "You still want to go with me?"

He raised his brow. "Why wouldn't I?"

"Cade, don't you get it? My father was a crook. My mother went from man to man as if she was changing her shoes. And you want to introduce me to New York society?"

"Do you think I'm a total fool? You're nothing like your parents."

"You don't have a clue what I'm like!"

"I know quite a lot about you," Cade said, the words playing and replaying in his head. Although he had no idea where they'd come from, they had the unmistakable ring of truth.

"I'm so ashamed of my parents," Tess said in a low voice. "I thought if I ever told anyone about them, I'd be dropped quicker than a rotten apple."

"You've got the wrong man."

"You're angry," she whispered.

"Not at you. At them. For the horrendous way they treated a little girl who was too young to defend herself."

"Oh." In genuine perplexity, she added, "Will I ever figure you out?"

"I'd hate to be too predictable."

Tess looked at him in silence. He crackled with suppressed energy, pullling her into his orbit by sheer force of personality. Predictable? What a joke. He'd listened to her sordid story without judging her, an act so unexpected that she was filled with gratitude. Not once in the last few minutes had he offered cheap pity; nor had he touched her. If he had, she might well have broken her self-imposed rule and wept all over him. Which wouldn't have been predictable, either.

Oddly the thought of going out this evening, of being surrounded by strangers and distractions, pleased her; right now she felt as though she'd been flayed, the memories crowding her mind too close and much too painful. "You're right, we'd better eat," she said, and managed a smile. "You'll like my dress—Susan picked it out because it's the same color as my eyes."

He should have bought her emeralds to go with it, Cade thought. But there'd be plenty of opportunities for that, too.

CHAPTER SEVEN

To say he liked Tess's dress was the understatement of the year, Cade thought, as he stood in the foyer and watched her descend the staircase. She was wearing a slender sheath of green, the taffeta skirt rustling as she walked, the tiny cap sleeves and abbreviated bodice heavy with gold embroidery. Her shoulders rose from it like polished ivory, topped by her flare of chestnut curls.

Desire slammed into him, rocking him to his foundations. Forcing his features to impassivity, he said, "Very nice."

"I'm not sure nice was the effect I was striving for."

He let his gaze wander from the toes of her gold spike-heeled sandals past her enticing cleavage to her exotic eyes, artfully shaped with eye shadow, her lashes impossibly long. "What were you striving for?"

"*Vogue. Elle. Flare.*" She grinned at him. "Aim high."

"Too much character in your face for a model—vapid, you're not. Before you wear that dress again, I'll buy you some emeralds."

"You will not!"

"You argue too much," he said, and held out his arm. "Shall we go?"

Tess hesitated on the bottom step. Cade looked disturbingly handsome in a black tux teamed with an immaculate pleated white shirt. Handsome, sexy and magnetic, she thought, with that undercurrent of animal grace that his highly civilized clothes only emphasized.

He knew more about her than anyone else in the world; and he hadn't run away.

He terrified her.

With a poise of which she was inwardly proud, she rested her hand on his sleeve. "My shawl is on the table by the door."

As he draped the swath of gold fabric around her shoulders, his fingers brushed her collarbone. A shiver of desire rippled through her. So that hadn't changed. If anything, it had intensified.

She glanced up and blurted, "When you look at me, what do you see?" Then she clapped her hand over her mouth. "Oh God, forget I asked that."

Cade let the weight of his hands fall on her shoulders and, for once, left his tongue unguarded. "I see a beautiful woman who isn't yet convinced she's beautiful. Who has no idea of the power she wields, and who might not wish to wield it even if she did know. A woman on the brink of the future..."

Startled, Tess stored the words away so she could think about them later. "You tell it as you see it."

"Is there any other way?"

"For you, no." Going on impulse, she reached up and kissed him, the softest of touches to his lips before she hurriedly stepped back. "You make me feel beautiful," she whispered huskily. "Thank you."

It wouldn't do to throw her over his shoulder and carry her off to bed—that went out of fashion years ago. With a huge effort, Cade managed to speak more or less normally. "Let's go slay 'em at the Met."

"You haven't even told me what opera we're to see."

"*La Traviata*. Star-crossed lovers."

Tess could have said, *I've never had a lover, star-crossed or otherwise*. But she'd done more than enough talking for one night; and wasn't her virginal state yet another of the secrets she'd guarded for years?

The chauffeur drove them to the opera house, where they were ushered into Cade's private box. The orchestra tuned up and the overture began.

When the curtain descended at the end of Act I, Tess wasn't ready for the break. Cade said, under cover of a storm of applause, "You like it."

"Oh, yes," she breathed. "So much emotion, and those delicious voices."

He'd never seen her face so open, so vulnerable. All her defences were down, he thought grimly. But he'd be the lowest of the low to take advantage of it. He'd damn well better find himself another woman, and soon; it was called self-preservation. "Would you like some wine?"

"I'd just like to sit here," she said. "But you go."

Good idea, Cade decided, and headed for the bar. However, at the end of the second act, Tess said, "I need to stretch. It's not going to end happily, I know...I wish it would."

"A glass of wine'll fix the blues," Cade said heartlessly.

He led her through the crowds in the lobby, introducing her to several people whose names she immediately forgot. Then a tall, slender blonde in a patrician white gown approached them. Ignoring Tess, she laid her hand confidingly on Cade's sleeve and reached up to kiss him. A kiss she'd intended for his lips, Tess thought; but Cade, at the last minute, moved his head so that the kiss landed on his cheek. "It's been so long since I've seen you, Cade," the blonde said. "Too long. We must get together."

"Hello, Sharon...may I introduce Tess Ritchie? Sharon Heyward, Tess."

Sharon assessed her with insulting brevity. "Hello," she said. "Are you enjoying the opera? The production's by no means as good as Zeffirelli's."

"As I've never seen it before, I can't compare."

"Your first visit to town?" Sharon smiled, her eyes ice-blue. "I thought you looked a little out of place."

"I grew up in Europe," Tess said, smiling back. "Amsterdam, Vienna, Paris. So it's pleasant to visit Manhattan with Cade."

Sharon's lashes flickered. "Cade, I'm in town until Tuesday. Surely you're not tied up all weekend."

Tied up, Tess thought with an inner quiver of amusement. The woman wasn't born who could do that to Cade Lorimer.

"Tess and I are leaving for France first thing tomorrow," Cade said easily.

Sharon's mouth tightened. Turning to Tess, she said, "Don't expect it to last, will you? Sooner or later, Cade always moves on."

"Leaving a trail of broken hearts behind him?" Tess said. "Somehow, Sharon, I don't think mine will be among them. But thanks for the warning...Cade, should we go back to our box?"

With an undeniable flounce, Sharon turned her back. "Nice to have met you," Tess added wickedly. Then, as she and Cade walked up the stairs, she hissed, "How often am I going to meet your ex-mistresses?"

"I wouldn't worry about it—you're more than capable of holding your own."

She was also, Tess realized, extremely angry for no real reason. "Or perhaps I shouldn't assume she's an ex? She didn't seem to think she was."

"Money, Tess, money. If I was down and out, Sharon would trample me under her Ferragamos."

"So why did you sleep with her?"

"You find me a woman who doesn't give a damn about the Lorimer millions!"

Tess gaped at him; it hadn't occurred to her that money could be, in certain situations, a liability. With painful truth, she said, "I'm no better than Sharon—I'm dressed from head to toe in stuff you paid for. And if you had your way, I'd be draped in emeralds as well."

He closed the curtains of their box with a decisive snap. "You'd be enjoying the opera just as much in the back row of the family circle," he said curtly.

"Huh…at least you didn't give Sharon the down-and-dirty about my life in Europe."

"Let's get something straight, Tess. We both come with a past. Yes, I've had affairs, of course I have. As for you, you're twenty-two years old, you've been on your own since you were sixteen—there've been men in your life and maybe we'll bump into one of them at the Paris airport."

She really should tell Cade the truth, Tess thought uncomfortably. She'd never get a better time than now. But as she opened her mouth, the conductor mounted his podium and bowed to the applause; and the moment passed.

As did the moment to ask Cade who would be his next mistress. He was on the lookout—he'd told her so.

She'd hate her. Whoever she was.

As the curtain rose on Violetta's bedroom, Tess's thoughts marched on. How could she hate someone she'd never met? It wasn't as though she wanted to be Cade's mistress herself. Dog in the manger, she thought, that's you.

Besides, Cade's a free man, who's doing Del a favor by

traveling four continents with you in his wake. You're nothing to him. Just one more beautiful woman in a string of beautiful women.

From the bed, Violetta began to sing, and Tess tried her best to sublimate her own feelings in those of the doomed courtesan. Gradually she lost herself to everything but the music. The tragic ending touched her to the heart, and she was very quiet as they walked out into the cool of evening, where water cascaded in shades of pink and gold in the huge fountain.

Violetta, so young and beautiful, had longed for her handsome lover with a depth of emotion that had been a revelation to Tess. But Violetta had died.

She, Tess, was very much alive. And hadn't Cade's kisses, passionate and passionately irresistible, also been a revelation, evoking cravings she hadn't known she was capable of?

She'd been fooling herself: she didn't want Cade to make love to another woman, or to find someone else to be his mistress. She wanted him to make love to her.

Her steps faltered. Revelation number three, she thought dazedly. Not that she had any idea how to seduce Cade.

"Tess, are you all right?"

"Oh—oh yes," she stammered, flushing as she realized that Cade's quizzical gaze was fastened on her face. Heaven knows what he'd been able to read there.

Nothing, she prayed. Her certainty that she wanted Cade for herself was too new, too raw, to bring it into the open. Let alone act on it.

She took a deep breath, calling on all her poise. "I loved the opera, Cade. Thank you so much for taking me."

"My pleasure," he said tritely, guiding her toward the waiting limo.

What would it be like to be Cade's lover? As she traveled round the world with him, would she find the opportunity—and the courage—to invite him to her bed?

She didn't do sex.

But would it be just sex with Cade? *Just* sex? What did that mean? Or would it be something else altogether, something operatic in intensity, unquenchable and all-absorbing?

There was no way Tess could tell, for she was operating from a basis of total ignorance. Although she'd read a lot of novels over the past few years, many containing sex, not one of them had prepared her for Cade Lorimer.

A few minutes later, when she walked into the foyer of Cade's brownstone, she was achingly aware of the silence. They were alone together. Cade's bedroom was upstairs. She'd checked it out this afternoon before he came home, had even sat on the bed on the dark blue spread and wondered—heaven help her—if he slept naked. She said raggedly, "I'm going to bed, it's been a long day."

He was tugging at his tie. "Whoever invented these damn things didn't have comfort in mind," he muttered. "Good night. Set your alarm so that we can leave by six-thirty tomorrow."

His mind wasn't on her, she thought, scurrying up the stairs. Or on sex. Which was, of course, a very good thing.

Tess dreamed that night about Opal singing a pizza ad at the top of her voice as she lay dying of an overdose, while Cory, in the next room, was fighting a duel with knuckle-busters…she woke with a start, sitting bolt upright in bed. Her heart was hammering in her chest and she knew from long ex-perience that she wouldn't easily get back to sleep.

So much for opera.

She pulled on a silk robe over her nightgown, and on bare

feet padded down the stairs. Surely she'd find hot chocolate, or at least tea, in Cade's highly impressive kitchen.

Rooting in the cupboards, she found an expensive brand of Amaretto-flavored cocoa. Trying to read the dates on the milk cartons, she propped the refrigerator door against her hip and stuck her head in the whole way.

"What's up?"

With a shriek of alarm, Tess backed up, bumped into Cade and turned in his arms. "I—I thought you were a burglar," she stuttered.

"I thought *you* were," he said dryly.

He was wearing a low-slung pair of sweatpants and nothing else. Dark hair tunneled from breastbone to navel; he was so close she could smell, elusively, a tantalizing combination of herb-scented soap and warm, male skin. Her palms were pressed to his chest; she could feel its muscled hardness through every pore, a sensation that made her melt like a candle to the flame.

The robe she'd flung on to come downstairs had fallen off her shoulders, and her nightgown was one of Susan's more minimal choices. Say something, Tess, she thought frantically. Anything. "I c-couldn't sleep."

"I thought I heard someone call out—that's what woke me."

Oh God. "I had a bad dream."

His arms tightened their hold. "I said you were safe here."

Safe, she thought. Was this his idea of safe? And was safety what she really wanted?

Violetta hadn't opted for safety.

Her heart was racing as though a wild bird was trapped in her rib cage; beneath her fingertips, his muscles were iron-hard. He was so beautiful, she thought helplessly. Why had she never realized that a man's body could emphasize so seductively her own femininity?

"Dammit, Tess, don't look at me like that."

"Is that the power you were talking about?" she faltered. "I feel so different with you, as though somehow you free me to be myself—and yet that woman is someone I don't even know."

Like a man driven to the brink, Cade sought out her mouth. She met him more than halfway, her lips parted, willing and eager. He nipped at her lower lip, then slid his tongue along its sweet curve, his hands skimming the length of her body under the slippery silk. Heat throbbed through her, swirled and shuddered. She moaned deep in her throat, arching against him. Then he plunged with his tongue and the world dissolved into nothing but desire.

It didn't take courage at all, she thought dimly, to be in Cade's arms; for it was the most natural place in the world for her to be.

She buried her hands in his hair, pulling his head down, aching for more, more, always more…and felt, with a thrill of possessiveness, the hard jut of his own needs.

He wanted her.

With a recklessness new to her, she rubbed herself against him and heard him gasp her name. He clamped one arm tight around her, pulling her into his body, the thin silk no barrier at all to an intimacy that drenched her in liquid fire. Drenched and destroyed her.

Clinging to him with the last of her strength, she dug her nails into the taut muscles of his shoulders. *Take me, take me,* she thought dazedly, and knew she was ready to travel to an unknown country. With Cade. Only with Cade.

Each tiny jab of her fingernails lanced straight to Cade's loins. With a muffled groan, he let his teeth graze the long line of her throat, thrown back, bared for him, before he dragged the thin strap of her gown down her shoulder. Her breasts' pale glimmer nearly drove him out of his mind. He dropped his head, tracing the soft rise of her flesh, then flicking her nipple with his tongue until it was rock hard. Until she was whimpering, incoherently begging him for more.

Muscle, blood, bone and sinew, he wanted her. Had to have her, had to satiate a need beyond any he'd ever known. He was drowning in her. Losing himself. He'd die if he didn't take her. Here. Now.

Somewhere, deep within, a red warning light flashed on. Drown? Lose himself? Die?

What the hell was going on? He'd never felt like this in his life. Never needed a woman as, right now, he so desperately needed Tess.

He didn't want to need her.

From the same deep place, he found the strength to drag his mouth from the sweetness and heat of her body, to fill his lungs with air and say in a voice that didn't sound remotely like his own, "I'm ending this. Right now."

She shuddered in his hold, opening green eyes that were drowned—that word again, Cade thought savagely—in desire. "I don't understand," she whispered. "What's wrong?"

How could he possibly explain something he scarcely understood himself? If Tess, at the age of five, had decided against love, hadn't he, equally young, decided against need? For as far back as he could remember, his real father had derided a small boy's need for love and approval; and Del had always kept him at a careful distance.

Surface relationships, Cade thought caustically, those were his specialty; and over the years they'd served him well.

He wasn't going to change, dammit. If Tess's body drove him too close to the edge, then he'd deny himself that body.

Simple.

"It's all wrong," he said implacably. "If we go to bed together, we'll both regret it in the morning."

Tess straightened, bracing herself with her palms to his bare chest, and said with ragged honesty, "I don't want you to stop—I won't regret it, I swear I won't."

The terror that had so puzzled him on the pebble beach of Malagash was gone; in its place was surrender, pure and simple. Cade said brutally, "But I will."

She flinched visibly. "So it was all an act?" she quavered. "No!"

"You're lying—you've got to be!"

"I'm not—some things you can't fake."

"Then what's going on? I don't understand…"

"I'd be taking advantage of you," he said stonily. When all else fails, fall back on clichés, he thought with savage self-derision.

"How could you take advantage of me when I've just told you I'm willing?"

Cade moved back so that Tess's hands fell to her sides. He should have pushed her away the first moment she backed out of the refrigerator into his arms, he thought furiously.

His willpower was impressive. But not that impressive.

Pride stiffened Tess's spine; like a cornered animal, she went on the attack. "Do you enjoy making women beg for your attention? For sexual favors? If so, I was right to despise you."

Then her eyes widened with comprehension. She gasped, "There's someone else. You've already found another woman. Of course—how stupid of me not to guess."

"Don't be—"

"I'll go through with this trip to France tomorrow because I don't want Del to be disappointed," she said raggedly. "But keep your distance, Cade—do you hear me? Or I'll damn well go back to Malagash on the first plane and leave you to explain why."

In a swirl of silk she marched out of the kitchen. The swing door swooshed shut behind her.

Cade let out his breath in a long sigh. Well done, he thought. He hadn't wanted to admit to himself, let alone to her, even the possibility that he might need her. So now he'd driven her away and—he wasn't completely blind—hurt her feelings into the bargain.

He was a brilliant CEO, yeah. But he was bottom of the class when it came to Tess Ritchie.

He might want to check his morning coffee for arsenic. On which less than comforting thought, Cade went to bed.

Alone.

CHAPTER EIGHT

At Charles-de-Gaulle Airport, Cade's rented Maserati was waiting for them; it was scarlet. The color of passion, he thought. The color of blood.

Ever since they'd left Manhattan for the airport where his personal jet had been parked, Tess had maintained an icy silence, sleeping her way across the Atlantic, now ignoring him as if he didn't exist. As the valet loaded their suitcases into the trunk, he climbed in and turned on the ignition. Two could play that game, he thought vengefully. Besides, driving in Paris always took his full attention.

As a couple of taxi drivers intent on mayhem swerved in front of him, she didn't even flinch. Her defenses were firmly in place and he thoroughly disliked being ignored.

You're not used to it, Cade. Your other women spent their time falling all over you.

Unlike Tess.

He covered the seventy or so kilometers to the château in record time. As he turned into the long driveway through imposing wrought-iron gates, their pale stone pillars topped with heraldic knights in armor, he said, "Welcome to Château de Chevalier."

"Thank you," Tess said coolly. She was determined not to

be impressed. But after the car had wound through a dense forest, which opened into formal gardens of clipped shrubbery and autumn flowers, she saw the château and gave an involuntary gasp of pleasure. It was riding the banks of the river in creamy splendor, its Renaissance turrets and windows shining in the early evening sun.

A palace out of a fairy tale, she thought, where all the endings were happy.

There'd be no happy endings for her.

"The tufa cliffs are to our left," Cade said. "Caves were dug into them generations ago, for aging and storing the wine. The vineyards are behind the château. It's a good time to be here. Some of the early-ripening grapes are nearly ready to be harvested, others are waiting for the first frost...we'll get rid of our stuff, you can change into something less formal, then I'll take you around. I haven't been here for two months, so I have a lot to do."

As he spoke of the harvest, his voice had warmed. So he cared, she thought, and blurted, "Learning the complexities of winemaking will be a breeze compared to understanding you."

"Then you'd better stick to the wine," Cade said.

Stifling both pain and anger, she did just that, until her brain was stuffed with a wealth of information about pruning, tannin content, Sancerre, rare vintages and wooden vats.

Somehow, the day had fled and it was evening. Wriggling her shoulders to rid them of fatigue, Tess followed Cade out into the courtyard. A full moon had risen through the trees, the walls of the château a ghostly white, poised over the still waters of the Loire. She said, "We haven't even touched on the marketing aspect of the vineyard."

"We'll do that tomorrow morning. It's a science in itself."

"Just don't let me do so much tasting tomorrow," she

remarked, picking her way over the cobblestones with exaggerated care. "I've never had much head for drink."

"You're cut off." Moonlight gleaming in his hair, he said abruptly, "I'd like us to walk some of the rows before we have dinner. Because, in the end, it's the grapes that count."

She was beginning to like him, Tess thought blankly. The depth and acuity of his knowledge, the respect and affection that the workers held for him: they were as real as the *parterres* with their well-tended blossoms, and the bronze statues reflected in stone-edged pools.

She was a long way from home.

Impulsively she said, "I'd rather be here than in the library on Malagash Island. I guess I'd outgrown safety and didn't even know it."

Cade stopped in his tracks. "You have this continual capacity for taking me by surprise."

"I bet Sharon never took you by surprise."

"Not once…you didn't like her any more than she liked you."

Without finesse, knowing the question was too important for her to hedge, Tess asked, "Is she going to be your mistress again?"

They'd climbed the slope behind the château. Rows of vines ranged the hillside, the canes heavy with grapes. Cade said, "These rows are Sancerre. Over there are Bourgueil."

"Is that a polite way of telling me to mind my own business?"

"I won't get involved with Sharon again."

Involved, Tess thought, what a horrible word. And used it herself. "Are you involved with anyone else yet?"

"What is this, an inquisition?"

"It's a straightforward question," she said, hoping he couldn't hear the sick pounding of her heart.

"No. Not yet."

So she had her answers. Glancing around at a world bathed in the moon's pale radiance, Tess realized with a tightening of her nerves how isolated they were up here, out of sight of the château and the outbuildings of the vineyard. She stooped to admire the carefully spaced bunches of grapes on the vines, taking a moment to gather her courage. Then, standing tall, she looped her arms around Cade's neck and kissed him full on the mouth.

Stepping back, she said, "I did that because I wanted to. Not because you're rich."

A breeze stirred her hair. An owl hooted from the forest, hauntingly sad; her heartbeat was like thunder in her ears, so loud she was sure the owl could hear it. Cade was standing dead-still, and as the seconds ticked by, the gamble she'd just taken seemed more and more foolhardy.

Anyway, it had failed.

Then Cade brought his hands up and cupped her face, his fingers digging into her skin. His gray eyes hard, he said, "In the long run, I'll hurt you, Tess. You're not the type for a casual fling and I'm not into commitment. Never have been."

"So do we do nothing because we're afraid of being hurt?" she cried. "That's what my life was like for the sixteen years I lived with Cory and Opal. Smooth the troubled waters. Keep a low profile. Don't rock the boat. I lived every cliché in the book, over and over again—until I was sick of them. But now I'm ready to take a few risks. After all, I'm here in France with you, aren't I?"

Her skin was cool to his fingertips, smooth as the finest silk. And wasn't he being offered, freely, the woman he'd ached to bed ever since his first sighting of her on a rocky beach in Maine?

He'd be a fool not to take her.

He said harshly, "So this isn't related to the fact that I'm a billionaire?"

"No!"

The words forcing themselves out, their raw truth roughening his voice, Cade said, "You can't be bought, Tess. You know it, and so do I."

Her eyes jerked to meet his own. "Do you mean that?"

"Yes," he said shortly. "Can't you tell? Or do you disbelieve everything I say?" Then, to his horror, he saw that her eyes were brimming with unshed tears. "For God's sake, don't cry—I meant it as a compliment."

She blinked furiously. "You trust me," she gulped, "that's what you're saying. And I never cry."

"You're giving a damn good approximation."

"It's so stupid—way back, when we were eating dinner at the hotel on Malagash, I was doing my level best to convince you I was after every cent you and Del ever earned. But now I'm nearly in tears because you understand that what's at stake here has nothing to do with money. Absolutely nothing."

So had he finally, Cade wondered, found a woman who didn't see him as a walking bank account? He said tersely, "This doesn't change the way I feel about anything long-term. Falling in love isn't an option. Marriage certainly isn't."

She raised her chin defiantly. "Mistress is an okay word."

"As long as you're sure of that."

"I'm sure." Her lips, those delectable lips, curved in a slow, provocative smile. "I'm beginning to think you're the one who's afraid of risk, Cade."

"Are you calling me a coward?" He whipped his arms around her waist and pulled her toward him. Her eyes widened and her smile vanished; her body was suddenly rigid.

"I take it back," she said, keeping her voice level with a

huge effort. She was the one who was afraid; and was desperate to keep that fear to herself.

Take the initiative, she thought. Before you run like a rabbit.

She let her palms slide up his chest, feeling through his shirt the heat of his skin, the hardness of bone and muscle. Feeling, distantly, the first stirrings of desire. She lifted her face, her lips parted, and with mingled excitement and terror watched his eyes narrow with purpose, points of fire in their dark centers.

He said with ferocious intent, "I've waited too long for this." Then his mouth plummeted to hers, his tongue lacing itself with hers, plundering her, robbing her of everything but a fierce, shocking need.

Somehow, from depths she hadn't known she possessed, Tess answered him with a hunger that matched his own; for if he had plunged to her mouth like a peregrine to its prey, then she was his mate, his equal. So she met him, fire with fire; and felt his arms tighten around her waist, hauling her into him, hip to hip.

She was burning all her bridges, she thought dimly. Which was another cliché. She was abandoning any notions of safety to embrace a man who would lead her into an unknown country…

Her response had rocketed through every cell in Cade's body. Holding to a vestige of control—for had he ever lost it so fast?—he slid his lips down the pale column of her throat to the little hollow at the base of her throat, and felt her pulse skitter under his tongue. "So you like that," he muttered hoarsely, and without waiting for a reply, pushed her jacket aside to find her breast, his breath catching in his throat as she shuddered with desire.

"I like it," she said weakly.

"I wouldn't want you to be in any doubt." With lightning speed he lifted her off her feet, pulling her into his body, and kissed her again, kissed her as though he'd been waiting all his life to be with this one woman in the moonlight beside an ancient river.

Her little gasp of shock was smothered by his mouth. He demanded and took, he sought and coaxed, and only when he felt her surrender in every bone of her body did he lower her to the ground.

Tess lay back, the long rows of grapes enclosing her, the darkly luminous sky over her head. Cade's big body was hovering over her, covering her; never had she felt so purely feminine, yet so certain of her own power. She opened her arms to him, welcoming his weight, his warmth. His face closed off the sky and his lips, once again, drank deep of her mouth.

Far away, the owl hooted. Cade barely heard it. He was steeped in the woman embracing him, his control shattered, and still he took and still she answered him, kiss for kiss, caress for caress. He tore her jacket from her shoulders, letting it fall back on the clipped grass, and to his huge gratification, felt her fingers fumble with the buttons on his shirt. As her fingers tangled themselves in his body hair, then swept over his nipples, he juddered in response.

His own jacket joined hers on the ground. Ripping at the buttons, Cade tore her blouse away from her body; her breasts, cupped in white lace, made his breath hitch. Swiftly he undid the clasp on her bra, gazing at her in a passion of pleasure and hunger before dropping his head to seek out her breasts' rosy tips with tongue and fingers.

She bucked in his hold, her sharp cry of delight inflaming him. Distantly he felt her yank his shirt down his back and take his bare shoulders in her hands, clasping them as though she never wanted to let him go. "You're so beautiful," he muttered, "so goddamned beautiful…I want to see you naked."

He raised his head, kissing her again, laving her tongue with his and plundering all the sweetness of her mouth. Then he pulled off his shirt, tossing it toward the vines.

Cade's shoulders gleamed in the moonlight, broad, tautly muscled; had she ever seen anything so beautiful, so infinitely desirable? And if he wanted her naked, then naked she would be. Her fingers trembling, passion conquering shyness, Tess unbuttoned her slacks and lifted her hips in a single graceful movement to ease them from her body.

Her legs, so long, so slender, flooded Cade with primitive possessiveness. She was his. Only his. With brutal strength, he ripped her bikini panties down her hips. She kicked them off, her hands instinctively covering herself.

"Don't be shy…there's no need."

"But I've—"

Stopping her words with his mouth, Cade drank deep. Then, lifting her hands one by one, he kissed her palms; from there, with mouth and hands, he began exploring the silken smooth curves and hollows of her body, from throat to collarbone to breast to navel. She was trembling all over, whimpering his name, and all he wanted to do was bring her pleasure. He slid down her body, parting the damp pink petals of her flesh, then stroking them rhythmically, erotically.

Swamped with sensation, Tess gasped in shock and delight, her body arching, her nails digging into his bare shoulders. "Cade, don't stop," she muttered, "please don't stop…"

Then Cade felt the climax seize her, feral, lethal, her broken cries echoing in his ears as she tumbled over the edge. Swiftly he gathered her in his arms, her body boneless, her heartbeat like a trip-hammer against his rib cage.

"Cade," she whispered again, "oh, Cade…"

He traced the long curve of her belly, clasped her by the hips and lifted her into his erection, flame shuddering through his limbs, primal and unstoppable. "There's more," he said hoarsely. "God, how I want you!" And kissed her again, ravaging her mouth.

She wrenched free, her breathing ragged. "I want you so much, beyond anything I've ever known…but be gentle with me, won't you? I've never done this before…it's all new to me."

His heart stopped in his chest. Riveted to the ground, he lashed, "What do you mean?"

"I'm a virgin," she said, a flush rising in her cheeks. "I should have told you before, but somehow the time never seemed right to—"

"A virgin?" he repeated blankly, a chill rippling down his spine.

"I've never even kissed anyone the way I kiss you. Let alone the rest…why are you looking at me like that?"

"Why didn't you tell me after the opera? We were talking about our pasts, I told you about the women I'd been with."

"I should have, I know. But you had so much experience and I had none. Absolutely zero. It's no big deal, Cade, it's not as though I've done anything shameful. Just the opposite, in fact."

He reached over and grabbed a fistful of their clothes. Then he surged to his feet. Roughly he hauled her up to join him. "Here, get dressed."

"What are you talking about? I don't want to."

"This isn't going any further—it went too far as it was."

"Don't treat me like a child!"

"I don't do virgins," he said coldly. "The women I bed know the score."

She said incoherently, "You're behaving like those job ap-

plications where you have to have experience to get the job—
yet the job's the only way to get the experience. Don't you
understand? I'm trusting you. With my body. With myself.
Surely I don't have to spell it out?"

"The other thing I don't do—as you know—is commitment," he grated, buttoning up his shirt. His reasons were
deep-rooted, powerful and profoundly private; the last person
he'd share them with was Tess. "I'm not into long-term. Hell,
Tess, do *I* have to spell it out? How can I have a temporary
affair with you? Apart from being a virgin, you're part of the
family. *Oh, by the way, Del, I initiated your granddaughter
into sex while we were away. Not going to marry her, of course,
but it was fun while it lasted*—is that what you're suggesting?"

"Del's got nothing to do with this," she seethed. "It's *my*
body. I do with it what I choose."

"Not with me, you don't."

She stamped her foot. "How dare you treat me this way, as
though I'm not capable of making up my own mind?"

The moonlight fell softly over her bare breasts, for she'd
disdained to put on her blouse. His whole body was one big
ache of frustration and lust. Fighting to subdue an anger that
he knew was out of all proportion, Cade said flatly, "Quite
apart from any other considerations, I'd be taking advantage
of your inexperience. When you get married, you'll want—"

"Married?" she interjected furiously. "After living for sixteen
years with Cory and Opal, you think *marriage* is on my list?"

"If it isn't, it should be. You can't let them run the show."

"I will if I want to," she retorted. "So why don't you want
to get married, Cade? Del and your mother loved each other—
you had the best of examples."

"Too constricting," he said evasively. "Too predictable, too
dull. I like variety. Playing the field."

She winced. "With me as just one more player."

He pulled on his trousers and shoved his shirt into his waistband. Tess was different. That was the whole problem. Just by being herself, she overturned all his rules, made nonsense of them.

She was also a virgin.

"Get dressed," he repeated, his voice unyielding.

Tess's shoulders sagged. "I've run out of arguments," she said helplessly. "It's like battering my fists against the walls of the château."

He glanced around at the silent rows of canes with their precious burden of grapes. "We should never have come up here."

So briefly she could have imagined it, he looked as though he was being torn in two; but then that illusory flash of pain was gone. She hardened her heart. She wasn't going to feel sorry for Cade Lorimer.

She wasn't going to feel sorry for herself, either, she thought forcibly, fumbling to do up her blouse. No, sir. She was going to dump all the rules she'd come up with over the years to keep herself safe, and live life on her own terms.

Starting tomorrow, she'd learn everything she possibly could about running a vineyard, and when she got back to Maine she'd ask her grandfather if she could have a job here.

Ask? No way. She'd demand he give her the job.

On the sole condition that Cade Lorimer never be allowed near the place.

It was a condition she'd insist on, Tess thought three days later, as the plane touched down on the runway in Venice. In the last seventy-two hours, she'd concentrated to the best of her ability and absorbed information through her pores. But the whole time, Cade had avoided her assiduously, delegating her education at the vineyard to his underlings whenever possible; on the rare occasions when he'd been forced to speak to her, his frosty politeness had been far worse than outright rudeness.

She should have been happy to have seen so little of him, she thought, unlatching her seat belt. Among the grapevines in the moonlight, hadn't he treated her like a teenager who didn't know her own mind? She hated him for that callous dismissal, of course she did.

Or did she?

She wasn't happy. She was unrelentingly and acutely miserable instead. If *La Traviata* had shown her the power of emotion, the aborted lovemaking in the vineyard had taught her all too much about desire, and its dark companion, frustration.

She still wanted to make love with Cade, lose her virginity with him, take that enormous leap into physical intimacy with him. He was indeed, as she'd recognized instinctively on the pebble beach at Malagash, her fate.

None of this made any sense, logically. Why would she still want to make love with a man who'd turned her down as casually, as cruelly as if she were one of the château's marble statues?

But then, *La Traviata* hadn't made much sense, either.

What made even less sense was the way she missed Cade's companionship and laughter, the warmth of his rare smiles, his touch. At the château she'd dreamed about him every night in her big four-poster bed, embarrassingly erotic dreams charged with emotions that each morning left her heavy-eyed and heavy-hearted. Day by day, her unhappiness had intensified; now, as she stood up and stretched her legs, she knew she was dreading their stay in Venice.

She soon discovered that she and Cade were staying in a luxurious DelMer hotel on one of the small islands in the lagoon; from her window Tess could see the nearby island of Burano with its brightly painted houses and wooden fishing boats. Obediently she toured the hotel with Cade, learning what went on behind the scenes to produce a seemingly effortless level of comfort and service for the guests.

It was interesting, and often an eye-opener; but it didn't captivate her as the vineyard had. Once again, though, Cade treated his employees with respect and genuine warmth: an attitude that emphasized, all too cruelly, the way he was treating her. Again, the anger she'd been aware of ever since Cade had ordered her to put on her clothes—ordered her as if she was a child—flicked along her nerves.

Anger felt better than misery.

At the age of sixteen, she'd taken control of her destiny. Wasn't it time she did the same again? Be damned if she'd be his victim, helpless, suffering in silence.

Fine words. But how was she going to put them into effect?

Midafternoon, when they took a break, she said to Cade with a casualness that, even to her ears, didn't ring true, "My brain's in overdrive, I can't do any more today…will you arrange for me to have a gondola ride on the Grand Canal?"

"I can take you by water ferry to far more interesting places."

"Tomorrow, perhaps. For now, I'd like to be an ordinary tourist. You don't have to come," she finished, risking a dart of sarcasm, "I wouldn't want to bore you." If he didn't come, she'd take it as an omen; and cancel—or at least delay—her ill-formed plan.

He could hardly deny her, Cade thought, for he wasn't blind to how hard she'd worked the last four days. Nor had she made any effort to reopen that disastrous moonlit conversation between the silent rows of vines: for that alone she deserved to ride a dozen gondolas. "I'll come," he said brusquely. "We'll have dinner in a little restaurant I know near the Rialto Bridge—you can sample Italian wine for a change."

So the die was cast, Tess thought with an inward shiver. Hadn't she known all along that Cade would accompany her? To keep her safe. Choking back a giggle that might have bordered on hysteria, she wondered if she'd have the nerve to go through with her plan.

The risk was astronomical, the chance of success...she had no idea if she'd succeed, or what would be the cost if she did.

But she couldn't go on as she was.

CHAPTER NINE

IN THE hotel bedroom, Tess took one of her dresses off the hanger. It was long, flowing and ultrafeminine, in a soft shade of tangerine: sexy without being too obvious about it. Her pretty sandals were encrusted with crystals, and she inserted delicate crystal earrings in her lobes. Then she added makeup to enhance her eyes; her hair was a knot of curls with tendrils that sculpted her cheeks, and a warm tangerine lipstick flecked with gold coloured her lips. War paint, she thought; and in a surge of cold terror wondered—when the time came—if she'd dare embark on this particular battle. Let alone win it.

*I'm not one of Cade's typical women, and I know he wants me…*keep that in mind, she told herself fiercely. After taking several deep, steadying breaths, she left her room and floated down the winding staircase to the lobby.

As always, her beauty struck Cade like a physical blow. More than one male head turned to watch her progress, he noticed with a possessiveness that was scarcely appropriate. He walked forward to meet her. "I found this shawl in the boutique," he said, "it can be cool on the canal."

The shawl was woven of the finest wool, a creamy-white that reminded her of the stone walls of his château. "It's lovely—thank you," she said with unaffected pleasure.

Sharon would have turned up her well-bred nose at so simple a gift. But Tess was wrapping herself in the shawl, stroking its soft folds. She's not for you, Cade thought viciously. She's a virgin. Out of bounds.

They traveled to Venice, *La Serenissima,* by water ferry, then boarded the gondola Cade had reserved; the gondolier was dressed in a striped shirt and straw hat. Tess sat on a fat cushion, facing the six-pronged, iron *ferro* on the stern. She was also facing Cade, impossibly handsome, impossibly sexy Cade.

The long wooden oar splashed peacefully in the water. Cade interjected the occasional explanation: of the colorfully striped mooring poles outside the *palazzi;* of the Gothic splendor of Ca'D'Oro; of the origin of the Church of the Salute, bathed in a fiery sunset. He was more relaxed than she'd seen him in days, she thought; and was glad she'd suggested this simple outing, even though her motives were suspect. Besides, he was speaking to her without that deadly politeness that had so crushed her spirits.

As the gondolier serenaded her in Italian, the glorious architecture further distracted her from her nervousness. The plan, after all, didn't have to be implemented until after dinner.

"I'm having a wonderful time, Cade," she said impetuously. "The canal's so evocative of the past. So romantic."

"It smells," Cade said pithily.

"You've got the soul of a businessman."

"I am a businessman." He gave her one of his rare smiles, producing an armload of yellow roses from behind his seat. "So I should toss these? They were intended as an antidote to the smell."

"You arranged for them to be here?" she said, charmed, burying her nose in the silky petals. "That was sweet of you."

In front of his eyes, she'd changed from the strictly businesslike partner of the last few days to the desirable and all too approachable woman he'd so nearly seduced at the vineyard. Cade's loins tightened. Furious with himself, he pointed out a *fondaco*, a twelfth century warehouse, and told her a little of its history. But she was still cradling the roses, her cheek brushing the delicate blooms seductively, her lips gently curved.

To his infinite relief, he realized they'd reached their destination. The gondola bumped against the mooring, then they walked along a crowded street past faded old buildings to the restaurant. Cade had chosen small and intimate, rather than imposing. Bad mistake, he thought, watching candlelight flicker over Tess's features at their secluded table. He said at random, once they'd chosen their meals, "The gondolier was pleased to be given the roses."

"After he told me his wife was pregnant, I wanted to do something for him—you didn't mind?"

He shook his head. Her lovemaking, inexperienced though it had been, had had that same generosity: a thought Cade squashed as soon as it surfaced. One more day at the Venetian hotel, a quick side trip on the way home, then they'd be back on his own turf. Maybe there it would be easier to keep his hands off her.

If the worst came to the worst, he'd call Cecilia. Or Jasmine. Or Marylee.

Tess's dress clung softly to her breasts; desperate to bury his face in her cleavage, so shadowed and enticing, Cade averted his gaze. The breeze on the canal had tousled her curls, and as she smiled at the waiter, her green eyes shone like jewels.

Desperate? When had he ever been desperate for a woman before?

Maybe abstinence was affecting his brain. Up until now, hadn't he always taken what he wanted?

Up until now, he'd always been in control.

"You look very fierce," Tess said edgily.

With a jerk, Cade came back to the present. "Sorry," he said with unaccustomed awkwardness. "How's the *insalata*?"

"Delicious," she said, spearing a sliver of sun-ripened tomato. "The dressing's to die for."

It's you who's to die for, Cade thought; and for a horrible moment thought he'd said the words out loud. Trying to pull himelf together, he began to talk about some of his early experiences in Venice, when he was wheeling and dealing to procure the renovation permits for the hotel.

To his relief, she declined dessert. He paid the bill and in no time was ushering her onboard the hotel's private water ferry. Half an hour, he thought. You can keep a lid on lust for thirty more minutes.

The soft putt-putt of the motor discouraged conversation. But the moon—the same full moon that had shone in the vineyard on Tess's naked breasts—was shimmering on the waters of the lagoon. At least he was sitting across from her; to have felt her thigh pressed to his would have been more than he could bear.

He'd never in his life been so glad to reach one of his own hotels. His jaw tight, he escorted her to the top floor, where her suite—next door to his—overlooked the spires and domes of the city. "I'll see you in the morning," he said.

"I'll look forward to it," she replied, gave him an enigmatic smile and closed the gilt-scrolled panels in his face.

In his own suite, Cade ripped off his tie, took a shower, which he tapered to cold, threw on sweatpants and turned on the TV. He wasn't going to get any sleep—he might as well brush up on his Italian.

Five minutes later, after he'd just poured himself a glass of Tuscan wine, a soft tap came at his door.

He hadn't ordered room service; and he had his own fax machine and laptop, so it couldn't be someone from the front desk. Puzzled, he peered through the peephole.

Tess was standing in the hallway.

Swiftly he unlocked the door. "Is anything wrong?"

"Aren't you going to invite me in?"

Her cheeks were pale, her eyes enormous. He took her by the elbow, drew her into the room and snapped the door shut. "Are you ill, Tess?"

Her robe was full-length, a virginal white. Beneath it, her nightgown reached to midthigh. It was diaphanous and not remotely virginal, he thought, his mouth dry. The plunging neckline alone was calculated to drive a man to drink. He said with impersonal crispness, "If you're not feeling well, I can call the hotel doctor."

In a staccato voice she announced, "I'm sick of being a virgin—that's all that's wrong with me, and that's the first thing I have to say."

Her chin was set at an obstinate angle, her face was still paper-white, and once again she'd taken him totally by surprise. Along with lust, admiration for her sheer effrontery entangled itself in Cade's chest. Doing his best to bank both down, he said, "You get first prize for initiative, I'll give you that. What's next on the list?"

"Don't you dare laugh at me—I'm scared out of my wits."

He was still holding her by the elbow, Cade realized, and dropped it as though it had scalded him. "How about a glass of Fontarollo?"

"I plan to stay stone-cold sober. I'm here to seduce you."

"You chose the right nightgown," he said nastily. "I turned you down—remember?"

"I sure do. But I've had three days to think about all your reasons, starting with Del. I'll never tell him I lost my virginity with you, and I don't see why you would—so he's out of the picture. That's the second thing on my list."

"Just how long is this list?"

Her eyes narrowed militantly. "I want to seduce you. And you want to go to bed with me, I know you do. That's the third thing—seducer and seducee."

"Maybe I'll be the one doing the seducing," he said with dangerous softness.

A hectic flush stained her cheekbones. "I didn't think this would be so difficult," she said wildly. "You can pour me a glass of that wine after all."

Turning his back, Cade filled a crystal, long-stemmed glass with ruby-red wine. Passing it to her, he said, "You're playing with fire, Tess—you know that?"

"I sure don't feel the slightest bit romantic." She took a big gulp of wine, plunked the glass down on the priceless antique desk and said, ticking off her fingers, "Del's no longer an issue. You're not involved with anyone else. And at twenty-two, isn't it time I played with fire?"

"I won't marry you," he said with no diplomacy whatsoever.

She tilted her chin even higher. "Affair versus commitment," she said, hoping she sounded more confident than she felt. "That's number four on the list. This will be a Venetian affair. Short and sweet. I don't want marriage, or anything approaching marriage, I told you that already. Freedom, independence and lots of space are what I need. You don't want marriage or long-term commitment—high potential for boredom and too predictable. So we're in total agreement."

It was ridiculous to be irked because her dislike of marriage equaled his own. Although, Cade had to admit, he was as far from bored as he could be, and once again she'd proven herself utterly unpredictable. She'd also had control of this discussion for too long. He said curtly, "If freedom means you can seduce six other guys along with me, the deal's off."

Her jaw dropped. "Are you nuts?"

"No. For as long as we're lovers—assuming that's what's going to happen—I'll be faithful to you. And I'll expect the same of you."

"Well, of course." Her eyes narrowed. "Although you're talking as though this affair's going to last a whole lot longer than two days."

"Who knows?" he said. "We might have to prolong our stay in Venice."

"Not indefinitely, we can't."

He raised one brow. "On the other hand, we might decide to leave tomorrow morning."

Her frown deepened. "Are you playing games with me?"

"It's a fine concept—A Venetian Affair. Should I choose to extend into An Adelaide Affair—which I admit doesn't have quite the same ring—I'll no doubt like that, too."

"You don't want commitment!"

"I want fidelity," he said in a hard voice. "And when either one of us decides to end this affair, we say so. Up-front. Whether that happens in Venice, Adelaide or Tierra del Fuego."

By now Tess was scowling. "You're doing your CEO act again."

"I'm the one calling the shots—that's the way I operate. So now it's my turn to ask a question. You're a virgin. There must have been men in your life, but for your own reasons, you didn't let them close enough to get to first base—"

"I'm not a baseball game—I'm a woman!"

"I'm very aware that you're a woman. Why me? Why now?"

"That's two questions," she said fractiously.

"So it is," Cade said, and waited for her to answer.

She took another gulp of wine. Folding her arms over her chest, she said rapidly, "I've been into control for as long as I can remember, probably because I had none as a child. But you and I—when we get within ten feet of each other, control goes into a tailspin. I'd never even felt desire for a man until I met you." She grimaced. "How naïve is that— and if you ever tell anyone, I'll kill you. But, Cade, whether I call it desire or lust or chemistry or hormones—or even romance," she added with a weak grin, "it's still the most powerful feeling I've ever experienced. And I want to act on it. Now. With you."

"Even though you're scared out of your wits."

Again she swallowed, the muscles moving in her throat. "Guess so."

"So you agree to all my terms? Fidelity, no commitment, and when the time comes, a good, clean ending?"

"Are you always this cold-blooded?"

"Yes," he said, "I am. Saves trouble in the long run."

"All right, I agree," she said in a smothered voice.

"Then what are we waiting for?"

He moved closer, watching her eyes dilate. The fear was all too real, he thought; if bedding her was to mean anything to either of them, it was up to him to lay it to rest. In one swift movement, he picked her up, holding her against his bare chest. "Come with me," he said.

She made an indecipherable sound in her throat; her body

was a bundle of rigid muscles, and he could almost feel her nerves vibrating. From nowhere came a flash of admiration for her courage. It was up to him to relax her, too. More strongly than he'd wanted anything for a very long time, he suddenly realized he wanted Tess to enjoy being in bed with him.

It was her first time.

So this lovemaking was more about her than about him, he thought, kicking open the bedroom door. Not totally altruistic—that would be pushing it too far, and he was no saint; but definitely focused on the woman in his arms rather than on his own needs. Wasn't that new for him?

He'd never gone to bed with her, and already she was changing him in ways he didn't understand.

He walked across the spacious, elegant living room into his bedroom, where through the open blinds moonlight splashed across the dark waters of the lagoon. Putting her down beside his bed, he stripped back the covers. "Lie down, Tess. I'll be right with you."

She sat down on the very edge of the bed, looking as though the slightest provocation would send her into full flight. Quickly he went to his toilet kit in the bathroom, found the foil envelopes and brought a couple back into the bedroom, laying them on the bedside table. "Oh God," Tess gasped, "I never even thought of that."

"Then it's a good thing I did," Cade said. Taking his time, he lit every candle in the room and pushed the door shut, so that the only light came from the moon and from the clustered blue and yellow flames.

Then he walked over to the bed and sat down beside her. She was clutching her robe to her chest, her hands white-knuckled. "I'm the one who instigated this," she blurted. "I don't know why I'm so scared."

He chafed her cold fingers. "You've never been with a man before—why wouldn't you be scared?"

In the dark depths of his irises, Tess could see tiny pinpoints of fire. To her nostrils, unmistakable, drifted the scent of his skin. She'd know him anywhere, she thought; and how could she possibly lose her virginity with anyone other than him?

She was behaving like a wishy-washy Victorian heroine who was terrified of her fate. Sitting up straight, she said, her voice scarcely quavering at all, "If you kissed me, I bet I'd feel better."

"You have the courage of ten lions," Cade said, lowering his head. His lips brushed hers with a sensuality that shivered along her nerves. She closed her eyes, the better to savor it, and felt his hands, warm and very sure of themselves, drop to her shoulders. With a small whisper of surrender, she brought her own hands to rest on his chest. The roughness of his body hair, the heat of his skin, licked along her nerves with delicate flickers of fire.

As though he was so closely attuned to her that he knew her every mood, Cade deepened his kiss, his tongue dancing with hers, his teeth grazing her lower lip. She let her palms glide over his chest, searching out the hard curve of rib bone, then the bumps of his spine: learning his body. Within her, heat leaped to flame. Against his mouth, she whispered, "I'm where I want to be. Here. With you."

"Right now, I wouldn't want you to be anywhere else in the world," he muttered and was suddenly devouring all the sweetness of her mouth in a kiss that ripped through her.

In a flood of gratitude and desire, she twisted in his arms. He pulled her onto his lap, her robe slipping from her shoulders. She shrugged out of it, longing to feel skin on skin, her breasts aching for his touch. As if he'd read her mind, he cupped their weight in his palms, teasing their tips until she threw her head back, whimpering his name.

"So beautiful," he said hoarsely.

Emboldened, she wrapped her arms around his neck, her legs around his body; and felt his hardness thrust between her thighs. He wanted her. But had she ever doubted that? Shuddering, her breath caught in her throat, she whispered, "We've got too many clothes on."

"Look down," he said.

He was stroking her breast through her diaphanous gown, her flesh like the ivory petals of a rose, the aureole a darker bud. Again she shuddered, wondering if she could die from sheer pleasure.

Gracefully she lifted her arms over her head; and watched him draw her gown up her body, then slide it over her head. His eyes drank her in, such an intensity of passion in them that, suddenly, Tess wanted to weep.

He slicked her nipples with his tongue. Sensitized, scorched, so aroused she scarcely knew where she ended and he began, she molded herself to him, clasping him by the hips, glorying in the jut of bone and tautness of muscle. With a gentleness that was laced with both daring and shyness, she edged the waistband of his sweatpants downward, and wrapped her fingers around his silken, heated center.

His face convulsed. He said roughly, "You destroy me."

"I—"

His eyes speared into her. Into her soul, she thought helplessly. "Tess, with me you're free—free to do whatever you want to."

"So making love can be another kind of freedom?"

He'd never thought so. "For you, right now, it can be," he temporized.

The words tumbled from her lips. "I've never touched a man like this. Never been naked with a man before."

It was an odd time for Cade to feel a sudden flick of fear. Pushing it away, he brought her palm to his mouth, smoothing it with his lips, feeling her fingers curl confidingly in his. Then he found the pulse in her wrist, feeling it flutter beneath his lips. "Do you like what we're doing?"

Her chuckle was spontaneous. "Like it? Understatement of the year! Oh, Cade, I didn't realize lovemaking was like this. So overwhelming, so powerful, yet there's a place for laughter."

"We've only just begun," he said. Swiftly he rolled over, carrying her with him. Stripping his sweats from his body, he kicked them aside. Then he drew her to lie beside him, length to length.

He was magnificent, Tess thought. Aroused. Male to her female. So focused on her that it made her tremble.

He was kissing her again, long, drugged kisses that throbbed through her until her whole body was liquid with longing. Lifting himself on his elbows, he hovered over her, his mouth lingering on her throat, on the delicate hollows beneath her collarbone, on the twin peaks of her breasts, swollen and agonizingly sensitive.

She arched, running her nails down his spine, feeling his thighs push hers apart and sink between them. His fingers, infinitely skillful, found her warmth and wetness, teasing, skimming, until it was unbearable; until she bucked under his touch; until the rhythms mounted to a climax that plunged her into that place where she was most intensely herself yet suffused with him in every cell of her body.

Very slowly she came back to herself. "You did it again," she whispered, sliding her fingers down his body, burying them in the tangled dark hair on his torso. "But I want more.

I want to be filled with you, Cade. To know what that's like…won't you show me?"

No barriers, he thought. Only trust. And felt again that fugitive nibble of fear.

Holding tight to restraint, wanting her to be more than ready when he entered her, he traced all her curves again with lips and hands. Her heartbeat was like a hammer in his ear, her quickened breathing and her roaming hands assaults to his control. But not until she was frantic with need did he deal with the foil envelope, then gently ease himself between her legs.

She was lying beneath him, her hair a chestnut swirl on the pillow, her eyes like dark pools in which he could drown. She grasped him by the waist, opening to him. Inexperienced, generous and heart-stoppingly passionate—she was all of those things, he thought. And, right now, she was his.

He thrust deeper. A flash of pain crossed her features, and was as quickly subdued. Braced, he held himself still with a huge effort. "I don't want to hurt you," he gasped.

She arched upward, gathering him in. "You won't. You aren't. Cade, take me, oh please…"

Deeper and deeper he thrust, until she closed around him like a silken glove, her inexpert movements inflaming him beyond bearing. But even then, he waited until he saw the same storm gather in her face, heard her broken cries and felt her inner throbbing. Pushed to the edge, to the very brink, Cade could hold back no longer. His own rhythms seized him, powerful and implacable. Watching her face, he fell with her; and spiraled to release.

Trying not to let his whole weight rest on her, he dropped his forehead to her shoulder, his chest heaving. Her skin smelled sweetly of lavender; he could feel her blood racing in her veins. Fighting for breath, he muttered, "Are you okay?" And raised his head for her response.

She took his face in her hands, her smile radiant. "I feel—oh, Cade, what words do I use? Joined to you. Fulfilled. Light as air, joyous as a rainbow." She laughed, a deep belly laugh that, involuntarily, curved his own mouth in response. "I feel wonderful, fantastic, splendiferous. If you want to add okay to that, go ahead."

"You're very good for my ego," he said dryly.

Sobering, she murmured, "You took care of me. Waited for me, made sure I was ready. Thank you for that—because it cost you, I could tell."

"You weren't supposed to see that," he said uncomfortably.

"Next time, I don't want you to hold back."

"I figure we could manage that in about five minutes—how about it?"

"Oh." She blushed entrancingly. "Really? That soon?"

"That soon."

"You still want me? I mean, I wasn't exactly—"

"You were perfect," he said briefly. "And in a few minutes, I'll show you how much I still want you."

She gave another ripple of laughter. "I like being in bed with you!"

"Good. Because I plan on spending a fair bit of time here in the next few hours. I don't have any meetings until noon tomorrow, and I'm sure the hotel can manage without me all morning." He eased out of her embrace. "I'll be back in a minute."

In the bathroom, Cade regarded himself in the mirror. Same face, he thought. Same body. But something was different. In the big bed in the next room, with a chestnut-haired woman, he'd shifted to a new place.

Tess's generosity, untutored and shy though it had been, was the essence of Tess: nothing to do with the fact that he was filthy rich. Tess hadn't been responding to the Lorimer billions; she'd been responding to him, Cade. So for him, also, this lovemaking had been a first time, he thought—the first time he'd ever been able to fully trust his bed-partner's passion.

Wasn't that, deep down, what he'd always wanted? Yet for some unknown reason, every nerve he possessed was on edge.

He took a couple of deep breaths, making himself relax. One thing he knew: the Venetian Affair was going to travel to Venezuela and Australia, and even back to Maine. It could take quite a while to get Tess Ritchie out of his system.

He wasn't done with her.

Not anywhere near.

CHAPTER TEN

CADE and Tess stayed for two more days on the little island in the Venetian lagoon. As she folded her clothes into her suitcase on the morning of their departure, Tess knew she wasn't ready to leave. Cade was shaving in her bathroom; she could see him through the open door. Naked to the waist. Lean, muscular and sexy.

She had sex on the brain, she thought irritably.

When they left here, was the affair over?

She'd told Cade it would be a Venetian Affair, finished when they left the hotel. Which just went to show how ignorant, how totally out of touch with reality a twenty-two-year-old woman could be.

While he hadn't exactly agreed to her conditions, not for a million dollars would she ask him if it really was over. Too humiliating.

Cade leaned forward over the sink and splashed water on his face. Catching sight of her in the mirror, he smiled at her, a smile that tugged at her heartstrings. She should end the affair now, she thought frantically, before she got in any deeper. Although wasn't she way over her head already?

Clutching the scrap of white nightgown she'd worn that

first night, Tess said, "We've spent a lot of time in bed the last couple of days."

He grinned, a piratical grin that caused—once more, she thought in horror—desire to uncurl lazily in her belly. "Be accurate," he said. "We've spent a lot of time making love. Occasionally we managed to do it in bed."

In a strangled voice she said, "In the bathtub up to our necks in bubbles. On the Aubusson carpet halfway under the table. Up against the wall right here in this room—we nearly knocked the picture down."

"I never liked that picture."

"Where haven't we made love?"

"The lobby?" Cade said with another of those devil-may-care grins.

"A girl has to draw the line somewhere," she said primly.

He laughed, striding back into the room, catching her by the waist and waltzing her around the very same carpet. In embarrassing detail, she remembered how she'd straddled him, ridden him, her naked breasts cupped in his hands...

Cade stopped by the chaise longue and looked her up and down. She was wearing a business suit tailored in dark green linen, her cream silk blouse very feminine, her exquisite legs in silken hose. "You look good enough to eat," he said, bent his head and kissed her.

So much for makeup, she thought distantly, wrenched her head free and heard herself say, "Is that our last kiss?"

His eyes narrowed. "What are you talking about?"

"We're leaving Venice."

"Are you telling me you want the affair to end?"

She couldn't bear it if it did. She tilted her chin. "Do you?"

"Where the hell have you been the last two days?" he said, exasperated.

"Men turn sex on and off. I've read about it in books."

If it hadn't been for the desperation in her voice, Cade might have laughed. Schooling his features to impassivity, he said, "You're stereotyping me—you're guilty of sexism. Oh, Tess, I'm disillusioned."

She glared at him. "Stop making fun of me!"

"Do *you* think I want our affair to end?"

"I—I guess not."

"Brilliant deduction," he said dryly. "If anything, I want you more now than I did two days ago."

The blush started at her throat and crept up her cheeks all the way to her hairline. "Me, too," she said in a small voice. "But we're going back home, we can't—"

"We can do what we like—we're consenting adults."

"A Venetian Affair, the sequel?" she said, engulfed in a flood of emotion that she hastily labeled relief.

"You catch on fast." He hesitated. "We've got to stop at another DelMer hotel before we head back to the States. But it won't take long. Then we'll fly directly to Kentucky."

"Kentucky?" she said, puzzled. "I thought we were going back to Manhattan first. Or Maine."

"Del deeded me his Kentucky thorougbred farm a few years ago. I just found out that the nearest neighbors are throwing a big party on the weekend—a good chance to introduce you to society."

"Thanks for consulting me first!"

"There wasn't time," he said impatiently. "Are you finished packing? We should leave soon."

Relief was swallowed in temper. "A Venetian Affair II—sequels can always be canceled."

"Yeah?" he said, plummeted to her mouth, laced his tongue with hers, and with one hand found the silken curve of her breast. And judged the precise moment when temper flared into passion.

He'd jammed her against an antique table bearing a priceless fourteenth century gold vase. Tess gripped him by the buttocks, thrust against his erection and wondered how she could have contemplated ending an affair that had wound itself around her, body and soul.

Soul? This was about her body, she thought wildly. And only her body. Then she stopped thinking altogether.

With an abruptness that shocked her, Cade pushed her away. He was breathing hard, his steel-gray eyes fired with emotions she couldn't have begun to guess. "The water ferry will be at the dock in ten minutes," he said. "I'll meet you in the lobby."

The door shut decisively behind him. Tess said a very rude word and shoved the nightgown into her suitcase. This affair was about sex, nothing but sex; it wasn't even remotely about her soul. She'd do well to remember that.

She marched into the bathroom and repaired her lipstick. Her cheeks were still bright pink, and her blouse was halfway out of her waistband.

What was happening to her?

It wasn't until Cade's jet landed at Barajas Airport that Tess realized their destination. She said uncertainly, breaking the silence between them for the first time since the jet had taken off, "Madrid? Why here?"

"The hotel's having staff problems—I'd rather deal with it face-to-face than by fax."

Madrid: the place where she'd been born, and where she'd lived for the first five years of her life. Not sure how she felt about being back, Tess sat quietly during the drive into the city. The baroque-style hotel was in old Madrid, near the Plaza Mayor; the lobby, with its silk wall hangings, gold-leaf columns and sumptuous paintings, took her breath away.

As always, Cade was greeted with respect and warmth. He held a low-voiced conversation with the manager, then turned to Tess. "There's a private room off the lobby, we'll have a snack there before we start work," he said.

She followed him past a huge vase filled with a bouquet of orange and purple birds of paradise and admitted to herself that she wasn't up for dealing with staff problems. Maybe she could suggest that she test the mattress in one of the rooms, she thought wryly. Alone. To catch up on her sleep.

Cade pushed open a door marked *Privado* and ushered her ahead of him. She walked in, then stopped dead.

A woman in an austere charcoal suit was standing on the Persian carpet. She was middle-aged, her sleek black hair wrapped in a chignon, her profile as imperious as an eagle's. All the color drained from Tess's face. Grabbing the door handle for support, she gasped, "*Bella!* But—they told me you were dead."

"They were wicked, selfish and cruel," the woman announced. "May they languish in limbo. May they burn in hell." A fierce smile lit up her face. "I am very much alive—as you see."

"It's really you? It can't be!" Then the older woman smiled again, a smile so full of love that Tess was wrenched backward through the years to a little girl in a playground whose nanny was smiling at her as she pushed her higher, higher and ever higher on the red wooden swing.

"You've grown up, *chica*," Ysabel said.

"Oh, Bella…" Swiftly Tess crossed the room and flung her arms around the other woman.

"I would have known you anywhere," Ysabel said raggedly, tears trickling down her cheeks. "I always knew you would be beautiful—I worried for you because of that beauty."

"You use the same perfume," Tess said in a choked voice.

Ysabel held her tight. "*Querida*," she murmured. "When I came to your lodgings that day and found you were gone, all three of you, in the night—no address, no word of where you'd disappeared—I was heartbroken. I tried to find you, but with no success. I missed you, *chica*, I missed you so much."

Tess straightened, gazing into Ysabel's dark brown eyes, the color of the chocolate treats she'd adored as a child. "I cried for days…until Cory finally told me you'd died. I believed him—why wouldn't I? But I shouldn't have."

"Cory Lorimer could say the sky was green and the whole world would believe him," Ysabel snapped, wiping the tears from her face. "It was his only talent."

"But—" Tess's brain finally began to work. "How did you get here? How did you know I'd be here today?"

"Signor Lorimer," Ysabel said, glancing over her shoulder at Cade. "He contacted me three days ago, told me he'd bring you to Madrid if I wished to see you again." She raised elegantly plucked brows. "See you? Of course I wanted to see you! His news made me so happy, Tess, so very happy."

Cade shifted his feet; he'd positioned himself near the door. When Tess turned to face him, her delicate features were glowing with a happiness that matched Ysabel's. But, he noticed, not even being brought face-to-face with a woman she'd loved, and whom she'd thought dead for years—not even that had made her cry. Why was she so afraid of tears?

Was he complaining? Hadn't he dreaded the prospect of two weeping females in the same room, he who never involved himself in the private lives of his women?

He said rapidly, "It was nothing. A matter of hiring a couple of investigators."

"You couldn't have given me a better gift," Tess said huskily. "Anyone with a credit card can buy emeralds. Or diamonds. Or even yellow sweetheart roses. But to find Ysabel for me...thank you, Cade. Thank you from the bottom of my heart."

She'd never looked more beautiful. With uncomfortable truth, his thoughts marched on. Over the years, he'd bought various women diamond earrings, bracelets and watches, forking over his credit card as casually as if he was ordering a martini. It was the way he operated, and it had served him well.

If pushed to the wall, could he remember the names of all those women?

No. He couldn't. What was it about Tess that made her so different from the rest? That made him behave so atypically?

He said abruptly, "We're booked into the suite on the top floor, Tess. Why don't you spend the day with Ysabel—there's a limo available for you near the front entrance. Then we could all have dinner together, and you and I will leave for the States tomorrow morning."

A martial glint in her eye, Tess said, "The appropriate response when someone thanks you is to say, *you're welcome, no hay de qué, no problem*...I could go on."

"You're welcome," he said dryly, and heard the common-place phrase echo in his ears. *You're welcome...you're welcome in my life.*

He was losing it. And Ysabel was glancing from him to Tess with a speculative glint in her remarkable dark eyes. With a brief salute Cade left the room, heading for the front desk and the far more manageable problems of a cashier who might have been dipping into the till and a chef who wanted a forty percent raise.

Yes, he was running away. So what?

* * *

At nine-thirty that evening, Tess and Ysabel were standing near the front door of the hotel, where the limo was waiting to drive Ysabel home to her charming little apartment with its flower-bedecked balcony; she and Tess had had lunch there. Throwing her arms around the older woman, Tess said, "*Buenas noches*…it was a wonderful day, Ysabel. And you'll come for a visit in October, won't you?"

"*Si Dios quiere…buenas noches, querida.*" Swiftly Ysabel tapped over the sidewalk to the limo, waved once and was driven away. Again, there had been tears on her cheeks.

Tess hurried back into the lobby. She knew exactly what she was going to do; and knew, too, that Cade would be busy in the kitchen observing the chef and his underlings at the height of dinner preparation for at least another half hour.

Upstairs in the suite, she lugged the chaise longue around so it faced the door. Next she showered, smoothing body lotion over her skin and painting her toenails a vibrant scarlet. Finally she took out the bag she'd carefully packed away in Venice, donned its contents and arranged herself on the chaise longue.

Nothing left to do but wait.

Outside the suite, Cade yanked off his tie. If he ever saw another temperamental chef in his life, it would be too soon. Trouble is, the man could cook like a dream—and didn't he know it.

He'd gotten a twenty-nine percent raise and had promised never to hold a deboning knife to the pastry chef's throat again.

All in a day's work. Cade turned the key in the lock and pushed open the door.

His heart gave a great thud in his chest. As he pulled the door shut and clicked the latch, the flames of perhaps a hundred candles wavered in the air. "Well," he said, "should

I call security? Tell them there's a strange woman in my suite? Although, come to think of it, the body looks familiar."

The woman on the chaise longue gave a smothered snort of laughter. She was wearing a Venetian carnival mask painted gold with black-rimmed eyes, high cheekbones and brilliant red lips; it was surrounded by a froth of scarlet net.

A net ruff circled her throat; a scarlet and gold fan had been strategically placed at the juncture of her thighs. Otherwise, she was as naked as the day she was born.

"Jazzy toenails," Cade added, leering at her. "Not bad breasts, either."

She raised the fan and waved it languidly over her mask. Again the candles flickered. "Or should I be the one to phone security?" she said, her voice muffled by the mask. "Would it be premature to warn them that I'm in grave danger? Of being seduced, that is."

He tossed his tie on the heavy mahogany table, following it with his shirt. Then he loosened his leather belt. "I'd say you have about five seconds to make that phone call."

"I could wait. A little danger adds spice to life," she whispered, her green irises gleaming through the eyeholes in the mask.

By now his heart was hammering against his rib cage. He kicked off his shoes and socks, let his trousers drop to the floor and yanked down his underwear. Fully aroused, he walked over to the chaise longue, knelt beside it and buried his mouth in the curve of her instep.

Her skin smelled delicious. Taking his time, he moved to her ankle, slid his lips up the inside of her calf and heard her gasp his name. Raising himself higher, he eased her thighs apart and eased his finger into all the wetness and heat he knew would be waiting for him. Her body arched, slender, smooth as silk, utterly familiar and unbelievably erotic.

She was moaning, her hips undulating, her rapid breathing all the encouragement he needed. Swiftly he rose to hover over her and plunged. As she cried out, rising to meet him, the fan dropped with a small clatter to the floor. Writhing, her movements driving him mad, she took him in, deeper, deeper, until he was lost. His hoarse cry of release mingled with her scream of ecstasy, their blood beating as one.

He let his head drop, feeling sweat bead his forehead. "You've wrecked me," he said.

She'd fallen back on the brocade pillows, her breasts rising and falling as she tried to catch her breath. "I have to take the mask off," she muttered.

"Can't take the heat?" He let himself rest on top of her, fumbling with the ruff and tugging it free of her throat. Then he reached for the elastic at the back of her head and eased the mask from her face.

She smiled at him with sudden, endearing shyness. "I wanted to surprise you," she said.

He gave a bark of laughter. "You more than succeeded— I forgot all about my homicidal chef."

"I aim to please," she said demurely.

She did please him, he thought, staring at her without really seeing her. She pleased him beyond measure. And what the hell did that mean?

A delicate flush wafted over Tess's cheeks; she had no idea what he was thinking. "I can't thank you enough for today," she said. "For the gift of Ysabel."

He flicked her nipple with his tongue, watching her eyes widen. "So is this about gratitude?"

"I don't know what it's about," she said with raw honesty,

reaching up to stroke his raven hair back from his forehead. "But I wanted to give you something in return for what you did today. Not something from one of the boutiques…that's too easy—and you have everything you need, anyway."

Did he? If that were true, why was he desperate to ravish the women he'd just ravished only moments ago? He said, "We could move to the bed. I'm the one in danger now—of falling off this goddamned chaise longue."

"It wasn't designed for two. Why do I have the feeling you don't like gratitude?"

He grinned at her. "Because I don't. Hell, Tess, of course I did my best to locate Ysabel. I'd have to have a heart of stone not to—she's the only person you ever loved."

"It was the most wonderful gift you could have given me." Then her own grin flashed across her face. "Glad you liked my mask."

"It was the fan that did me in." He stood up and lifted her into his arms. "Bed," he said. "Are any of these candles about to set the place on fire?"

"You and I are going to do that," she murmured, tracing his lip with her fingertip.

Sensation, raw and primitive, surged straight to his loins. His last thought, before he carried her into the bedroom, was that tomorrow he was going to buy her emeralds—because he wanted to make love to her when she was wearing nothing but an emerald necklace.

Would he ever have enough of her?

The day—or night—he thought with a touch of grimness, would arrive when he would have had enough of her. Or, for that matter, she of him. That was the way it worked.

Inevitable.

CHAPTER ELEVEN

THE next day, under a moody gray sky, Tess fell in love.

Cypress Acres was a sprawling expanse of rolling green fields, freshly painted white rail fences and groves of tall trees whose leaves rustled in the wind. And horses, she thought, getting out of the car to stretch the day's travel from her limbs. Like a woman hypnotized, she crossed neatly cropped grass and leaned on the top rail of the fence.

Mares were grazing in the field, lazily swishing their tails against the flies, their coats glossy with good health. Foals slept on the grass, frolicked on the hillside and nudged for their mothers' milk. When Cade came up behind her, she said dreamily, "I'd made up my mind I wanted to work at the château. But now I want to be a stablehand, and learn all about the horses."

"You can do both," he said, watching her rapt face.

"They're so beautiful."

He'd always loved Cypress Acres, ever since he'd taken it over on his twenty-fifth birthday seven years ago. "Have you ever ridden one?"

"Never."

"I'll give you a lesson before dinner—want to check out the barn?"

"Oh, yes."

"Let me go ahead and make sure the dogs aren't around." Her face changed. "How many dogs?"

"Three. Purebred German shepherds. Very well trained."

Something he couldn't decipher flickered across her features and was gone. She rolled her shoulders, as if trying to rid them of tension. "I'll wait here for you," she said.

Once Cade signaled to her from the door, she entered the dim, spacious barn, which smelled sweetly of hay and was immaculately clean. Taking her time, Tess went from stall to stall, rubbing aristocratic noses and doling out carrots. She met Zeke, the head groomsman, and won him over by her frank avowal of total ignorance and her wish to learn all she could in the next few days.

Ten minutes later, dressed in a pair of old jeans and a sweatshirt, she had her first lesson with a currycomb and a mildmannered gelding named BillyJ. Then she was put to work with a can of saddle soap and an old leather harness. Cade left her to her own devices and went inside the house to phone Tiffany's.

When he came back out, wearing jodphurs and well-worn riding boots, Tess was in the ring with the same gelding, as Zeke supervised her first lesson with the lunging line. While BillyJ wasn't about to break any of the rules, Cade could tell right away that Tess had an instinctive feel for the animal at the other end of the line, the kind of feel that couldn't be taught.

Bow-legged and grizzled, Zeke strolled over to the fence. "She's got the touch," he said briefly. "Thought I'd put her up on Arabesque."

"Good choice. Believe it or not, she's never been near a horse before today."

Zeke pushed back his greasy ball cap. "She listens," he said. "Doesn't forget what you tell her."

"High praise."

"We'll see if she's got lasting power."

Cade's conscience gave him a nasty nudge. It wasn't Tess's lasting power that was the issue, it was his own. Love-em-and-leave-em-Lorimer…he'd been called that ever since he was old enough to date. "I'd suspect she has," he said, and knew he was talking about more than horses.

Zeke shrugged. "You'll take Galaxy later?"

Galaxy was Cade's bay stallion. "After Tess has a riding lesson. If you can keep the dogs away from her, I'd appreciate it—she's got a real phobia."

"I'll only leave them loose in the barn at night. But we should introduce her to them."

When BillyJ was back in his stall, placidly munching hay, Cade said, "Tess, you have to meet the dogs, just in case you come across them unexpectedly. They're trained guard dogs, and once they know you're a resident, they won't bother you. Zeke and I will be here—you don't have a worry in the world."

She bit her lip. Nothing came without a cost, she'd learned that a long time ago. If, in order to spend time with the horses, she had to face three dogs, she could handle it.

"Okay," she said in a small voice.

"Zeke, would you bring them in?" Cade asked.

Zeke ambled off. Although Tess braced herself, when Zeke came around the corner with three large German shepherds on leather leashes, she shrank backward.

"You're safe," Cade said. "I won't let anything happen to you."

You don't understand the first thing about me… Again Tess bit her lip, forcing the words back where they belonged. Zeke brought the dogs closer. "Just let them sniff you," he said. "Spirit, Tex, Ranger—friend. Friend. Got it?"

Three tails wagged. Then Zeke wheeled in a half circle and led the dogs away. "That's it?" Tess mumbled.

Cade rubbed the tension from her shoulders. "To think I once called you a coward," he said wryly. "I should have been shot on the spot."

Her body jerked as though he'd hit her; her eyes were barricaded against him. "You did say riding lesson?"

"Anytime you're ready."

The riding lesson was a revelation to Tess. She sat quietly on the white mare named Arabesque, her hands relaxed on the reins, and before the lesson ended had mastered the art of posting in the saddle. As she slid to the ground, her smile was brilliant. "Can we have another lesson tomorrow?"

"You're going to be sore tomorrow."

"You trying to get out of it?"

"Ten a.m.—after you've cleaned three stalls and polished a couple of saddles. In the afternoon, I'll give you a crash course on the finances of breeding thoroughbreds."

"Slave driver," she said amiably, and led Arabesque into the barn. She rubbed the mare down, told Zeke she'd see him in the morning and trailed behind Cade to the house. It was an antebellum mansion, painted white like the fences, with a host of brick chimneys and mullioned windows shot with the golden rays of the setting sun.

As Cade opened the side door, she said, "You have such good rapport with Zeke—with all your employees for that matter—it doesn't fit your CEO act."

He gave a short laugh. "I worked on a cattle ranch in Argentina and a dude ranch in Montana—I know what it's like to look after other people's animals."

"You did?" Her frown deepened. "When? And why?"

What was the harm in telling her? "When I was twenty, I

traveled around the world for two years on a shoestring—no money other than what I earned with my own two hands. I loaded pulpwood in Alaska, sorted scrap iron in China, portered in the Himalayas—you name it." He shrugged. "You could say it was the making of me. It certainly shaped the way I run Lorimer Inc., and how I relate to my employees."

Tess said with painful truth, "Back in Maine, I accused you of living in an ivory tower…I'm sorry."

"Ivory towers, I'd be willing to bet, are dead boring places to live." He ushered her indoors. "You must be ready for a shower and dinner?"

Her mind still occupied with the image of Cade sorting scrap iron, she said absently, "More than ready—in Madrid it's eleven at night."

"Shower, dinner and bed," he said. "Maybe you should sleep alone tonight. Sleep being the operative word."

Tess stumbled on the staircase, forgetting about that younger Cade. Perhaps, she thought sickly, their affair had been a European Affair: fine in Venice and Madrid, but finished now that they were back on home territory. Scrabbling for a vestige of self-control, she said coolly, "I am quite tired."

"It's been a long day."

Cade was marching her along a dimly lit hallway lined with depressing portraits of family ancestors. Scurrying to keep up with him, Tess blurted, "Are you trying to break it to me gently?"

He stopped so suddenly that she cannoned into him. "Break what?"

"That the affair's over."

"All I want is for you to have a decent night's sleep!"

Her shoulders sagged. "So it wasn't just a European Affair—it's transatlantic?"

"Multinational, if we head out for Venezuela and Australia next week. This is the second time you've brought this up. Are you sure you don't want to end it yourself?"

"Yes! Or do I mean no?"

"What do you mean?"

"I don't want it to end!" Then she blushed, furious that she'd sounded so vehement. Pulling away from him, she muttered, "Well—that was a dead giveaway."

Unease now added itself to the stirrings of Cade's conscience. He said carefully, "I'm the first man you've ever made love with, Tess. Don't mistake it for more than it is, will you?"

He couldn't have given her a clearer warning, she thought, gazing up at him. "Don't fall in love with you—that's what you're saying."

"Precisely."

"I don't love you," she said sharply. "But when we're together in bed...we both call it *making love*."

Choosing his words, aware even as he spoke how bland they sounded, Cade said, "We care for each other."

"I like you," she said.

He should have expected her to speak her mind. "Liking's fine," he said. "Just don't carry it to the next step, that's all."

"I promise I won't," she snapped. "Where's the nearest shower? I stink of horses."

Cade opened the door to his left. "These are your rooms. Mine are next door. Bedroom, bathroom, balcony overlooking the rose garden—you'll find all you need. Dinner's in half an hour."

His smile was impersonal. From somewhere Tess dredged

up one that was equally cool and shut the door in his face, jamming the lock with vicious strength.

She'd gotten the worst of that discussion. So Cade cared for her. He cared for his Maserati.

Probably more. It didn't argue with him.

Why did she want to fling herself facedown on the bed and indulge in a storm of weeping? She never cried.

She went through every swear word she could think of in every language she knew. Then she had a shower and put on a slinky black dress that, unlike her homemade one, screamed haute couture. It also screamed sex.

After dinner, a meal where she ate sparingly because her appetite seemed to have deserted her, she pushed back her chair and said, her eyes glittering, "I think I'll take you up on that offer to sleep alone. Good night, Cade."

Cade surged to his feet. Candlelight, from the ornate silver candelabra placed at intervals down the mahogany table, burnished her hair and glowed on the soft swell of her breasts. He said, "If you're interested in sleeping alone, you chose the wrong dress."

Her nostrils flared. "I'll wear what I want."

He stepped closer, watching her fight the desire to retreat. "You want me," he said roughly.

"I want you to go straight to hell."

"Then let's go together," he said, and swept her up into his arms.

She kicked out at him, pummeling him on the chest with her fists. "Put me down!"

He thrust the door open with one knee. "Quit struggling," he grunted. "You're not going to win."

White-faced with rage, she seethed, "Because you're

bigger. Stronger. Tougher. Because you're a guy. Put me *down*, Cade."

So suddenly that she staggered, he dumped her, feetfirst, to the floor. Then he thrust her against the wall, took her chin in his fingers and planted a kiss on her mouth so searing, so torrid, that Tess locked her arms around his nape and kissed him back.

She was furious with him, she thought dimly. She wanted him. Oh God, how she wanted him...

He pulled his mouth free, then reached up and jerked her arms apart. "Now you can go to bed," he snarled. "Alone."

Rage scorched her cheeks. "What was that all about? Punishment because I dared to oppose the mighty Cade Lorimer?"

"I wish it was that simple."

"So what *was* it about?"

"None of your goddamned business!"

Hands on her hips, Tess glared at him. "I'm not the slightest bit in love with you—get that fact through your thick skull. In fact, at this precise moment, I don't even like you." His jaw dropped. "Oh," she said blankly. "So that's what's wrong—you're in love with *me*."

"I am not!"

In dulcet tones, Tess misquoted, "The man doth protest too much, methinks. Shakespeare. I'm a librarian, remember?"

Determined not to be outdone, Cade dredged his memory. *"I understand your kisses and you mine."*

"Love goes toward love... Romeo and Juliet."

A thing of beauty is a joy forever. He wasn't going to say that. Anyway, it was Keats. "Tess," Cade said, "in plain English, I am not in love with you. Got that?"

She staggered artistically, drawing the back of her hand across her forehead. *"A poor lone woman."*

Regrettably Cade laughed. "Oh sure. How about a compromise? We go to bed together and go straight to sleep."

"What are the odds of that?" she said, a gleam in her eye.

"Only one way to check it out."

"Your place or mine?" she said demurely.

He was still laughing as he ushered her into his bedroom. They didn't go straight to sleep; Cade had known they wouldn't. But eventually they did fall asleep, naked, tangled in each other's arms. And the next morning, at dawn, Tess woke to find Cade leisurely tracing the long curve of her spine with his lips, his erection pressed into her hip. She lay still, reluctant to let him know she was awake, her whole body in a trance of desire.

He was kissing her shoulders, pushing her hair aside to kiss her nape, his fingers seeking out the soft fullness of her breast. Slowly, sensuously, she turned over, opening her arms to him. In utter silence, he made love to every inch of her body. As though he was worshipping it, she thought. As though she was infinitely precious to him.

Or was her imagination working overtime?

The storm, inevitably, gathered them both, lifted them, then hurled them toward release. Still without saying a word, Cade enfolded her in his arms, dropped his cheek to her shoulder and drifted off to sleep again.

But Tess found herself wide-awake. Not moving a muscle, her body satiated, she gazed at his sleeping features. He had, truly, made love to her; there could be no other way to describe his generosity, or his attention to her every need.

She was the one who'd better phone security, she thought crazily, because she was in danger: in danger of falling in love with Cade. How could she make love with him, day after day, night after night, with such aching intimacy, and not fall in love with him?

She'd be a fool to do anything so risky. Sooner or later, the affair would end. Maybe not on this continent. Maybe not for weeks. But end it would.

Terror, her old enemy, seized her in its grip. She didn't want it to end. She couldn't even contemplate letting another man into her bed. It was Cade she wanted, and only Cade.

Now and—her mind quailed—forever.

That day Tess mucked out three stalls, watched Zeke apply strong-smelling linament to a swelling on the foreleg of a stallion called Hyperion and had a riding lesson at ten with Cade. Knee grip, use of the bit, pressure on the turns and this time a thrilling, although too brief, canter around the ring. She then rubbed Arabesque down.

After that, she worked a yearling on the lunge, closely supervised by Zeke. A brief lunch, then Cade took her through the account books, and introduced her to the intricacies of tracking a thoroughbred's lineage.

A shower had never felt so good. After dinner, in preparation for the neighbor's ball, she and Cade had a dancing lesson in the empty, echoing ballroom. She loved music and he had an innate sense of rhythm; her brow knit with concentration, she added the foxtrot and waltz to her list of new skills. Then she followed him upstairs to his room, changed and fell into the bed. "You haven't seen this nightgown yet," she mumbled. "I've been saving it up."

It was midnight-blue, see-through, so seductive Cade forgot his half-formed plan to cool their affair for now. But as he leaned forward to brush her parted lips with his own, her lashes had already drifted to her cheeks; her breathing deepened.

There were faint blue shadows under her eyes. Very carefully, Cade eased down beside her on the bed. Tess had solved any question of him implementing his plan by falling asleep.

He didn't know whether to be glad or sorry.

Tess woke sometime in the middle of the night. She'd been dreaming. The images fled as soon as she opened her eyes; but the dream's mood, its sense of entrapment, of fear and foreboding, lingered.

Cade was deeply asleep beside her, his hair black on the pillow in the light of a waning moon. One of his arms was flung over her ribs; against her back, she could feel the strong, steady beat of his heart.

She should feel safe with him so close to her; all she had to do was wake him and he'd comfort her.

What if she got used to asking him for help? What then?

Managing not to wake him, she slipped out of bed, found her barn clothes in a heap on the floor where she'd dropped them before dinner and got dressed. Trying to avoid floorboards that creaked, she crept to the door and slid into the hall. A bewigged ancestor with a pursed mouth stared at her disapprovingly from the wall.

The stables, she thought, that's where I'll go. The horses will make me feel better.

Her dream must have been about Cory and Opal; no one else had the power to so drench her in dread. But she wasn't in her parents' power anymore, she thought stoutly, checking that she had her keys before letting herself out the side door. Because of Del, she had money; because of Cade, she was learning about corporations, hotels, vineyards and thoroughbreds; and she'd reconnected with Ysabel.

She had choices now. As a child, she'd had none.

The night air was cool and damp, clouds smothering most

of the stars. Soft-footed, she walked to the barn, unlocked the grooms' door with her key and closed it behind her. A horse whickered a welcome, poking its head out of the stall. "Hello, Galaxy," she said softly and started over the concrete floor toward him.

In a rattle of claws, three German shepherds lunged around the corner and ran right for her. Even in the dim light, she could see their teeth, white, sharp and deadly. With a tiny gasp of dismay, she held her ground.

There was nowhere to run.

"I'm your friend," she squeaked. "Zeke said so."

The dogs surrounded her, avidly sniffing her sneakers and jeans. Their tails were wagging, she realized. Then the largest of the three sat back on his haunches, mouth agape as though he was laughing at her.

Her dog in Amsterdam, her beloved Jake, had had a strong streak of German shepherd in his mixed ancestry; his eyes had been filled with the same golden, alert intelligence.

Tess dropped to her knees. Tentatively she put out her hand to the dog's collar, angling the tag so she could read the name inscribed on it. "Spirit," she whispered, and patted him on the shoulder.

He swished his tail on the concrete floor. The other two dogs were busily nosing her shirt, and suddenly it was too much. In a great upsurge of memory, she put her arms around Spirit and buried her face in his fur.

The first sob pushed its way from somewhere so deep that, instantly, she was undone.

CHAPTER TWELVE

CADE wasn't sure what woke him. A sound? The sense that he was alone in the big bed? "Tess?" he said, wondering if she'd gone to the bathroom.

He was answered by the silence of a sleeping house. Sitting up, switching on the bedside light, he saw that the bed was indeed empty and that the untidy heap of Tess's barn clothes was gone.

Every instinct he possessed warned him to find her, and find her fast. He got up, threw on jeans and a T-shirt and headed out the door. He'd be willing to bet she'd gone to the barn, although he had no idea why.

The dogs, he thought with a stifled curse. Zeke had been leaving them loose in the barn at night.

He took the stairs two at a time and hurried out the side door. No lights in the barn, and not a sound from the dogs. If she wasn't there, where was she?

He unlocked the outer office door, where stud books were neatly arranged on the shelves and the small green lights on the computer shone coldly. The inner door, to the barn, opened smoothly.

Horror jolted through his body. The dogs had dragged her to the floor.

He leaped forward. But then, belatedly, he realized that she had her arms around one of the dogs, and that she was weeping. Weeping as though her heart was broken, he thought, and stopped in his tracks. He'd never heard such desolation, such profound sorrow—the sorrow of a lifetime, surely.

Two of the dogs raised their heads, and one of them trotted over to him, burrowing a cold nose into his hand. But the third dog stayed where he was, unmoving, for Tess was sobbing into his fur, her shoulders heaving.

Cade said quietly, "Tess, don't be scared—it's me." Then he knelt beside her and put his arms around her, turning her into his chest. Unresisting, her body shuddering in spasms of weeping, she fell into his embrace. Spirit nuzzled closer. Cade held on to the woman and the dog, knowing there was nothing he could do until she'd emptied herself of tears.

She never cried. She was terrified of dogs. Yet he'd found her weeping her guts out in the middle of the night, surrounded by three very large dogs, one of whom she was wrapped around as though she never wanted to let go.

Thank God he'd woken up; and he had the rest of the night to find out what was going on.

Gradually her sobs became less frequent, her body sagging against him in utter exhaustion. Fumbling in his pocket, he found a handkerchief and pressed it into her hand. "Blow your nose," he said. "Then I'll take you back to the house."

Head lowered, she scrubbed at her nose and wet cheeks. "I had a dog," she quavered. "In Amsterdam, the year I was sixteen. His name was Jake. Spirit looks like him."

All his senses on high alert, Cade said, "What happened to him?"

Her breath heaved in her chest. Gazing at the buttons on Cade's shirt, she said jaggedly, "Soon after I turned sixteen,

Cory's luck ran out. He was shot dead outside a drug dealer's only three blocks from where we lived. I heard about it and ran home to tell Opal. She was terrified. Told me to stay away from the flat for the next week, threw a couple of bills at me and said she'd meet me at the nearby hostel that night."

Tess drew another deep, shaky breath. "She didn't turn up that night, or the next two nights—she probably left on the first train the day Cory was shot."

Cade's breath hissed through his teeth. "When my money ran out," Tess said flatly, "I had nowhere to go. I was too frightened to go back to the flat. So I started roughing it on the streets. I found Jake the third day—he was a stray, hanging around a Dumpster. I panhandled at the station for the two of us, and for a couple of months it went okay. He was a big dog, wouldn't let anyone near me...so I felt safe."

"But you weren't."

"One of the local gang leaders had his eye on me. Ysabel was right—I was too pretty for my own good. I was saving for a train ticket to Den Haag, and I nearly had enough money. But one day when I went to the back door of a restaurant looking for a handout, Hans was waiting for me."

In the dim light, Cade could see her eyes were drowning in remembered terror. Tess at sixteen, he thought—the year the investigator hadn't found a trace of her.

"He grabbed me," she said in a rush. "When Jake went for his throat, Hans shot him. Full in the chest. But even then, Jake managed to knock Hans down." She stifled a sob. "I ran. Ran faster than I've ever run in my life, and by a miracle I managed to shake Hans off. I hopped a freight train that night and got out of town. The rest's history."

Cade said the obvious. "You had to leave Jake behind. You couldn't even bury him."

Her face convulsed. "Jake and Ysabel—they both loved me, and I lost them both."

"Jake saved your life," Cade said, throttling down emotions that threatened to choke him, for her bleak account had shaken him to the roots. "No wonder you didn't want anything to do with the dogs at Moorings. At the time, I misunderstood. You weren't scared of the dogs themselves—it was the memories that terrified you."

"When I reached Den Haag, I got a job washing dishes in a Chinese restaurant." She gave a watery smile. "From there, it was uphill all the way. Cleaning offices at night, ushering in a theater, making cold calls for a market agency...you name it, I've done it."

"How did you get to the States?"

"Housekeeper on a cruise ship." She hesitated, adding in a low voice, "I should have told you all this back in Manhattan. But I couldn't. I just couldn't."

He had to take that look off her face. Cade said calmly, "You could make a donation to an animal shelter in Amsterdam in Jake's memory—you can afford to do that now."

Her face brightened. "That's a wonderful idea—I'll do it."

Cade got to his feet, drawing her up with him. "You're exhausted," he said roughly. "Past time you were back in bed."

She looked right at him, her eyes like dark pools. "Thanks, Cade. For letting me cry. For listening."

He didn't want gratitude, that much he knew. His shoulders tight with tension, he said, "Do me a favor, will you?"

"Of course."

"Every day, write down some of the details of those weeks in Amsterdam. Describe where you slept every night, for instance. What markings Jake had."

She shivered. "He'd lost the tip of one ear. I'll never forget how he snarled when Hans grabbed me…."

"Tess, you got yourself out of Amsterdam and you made it all the way to Malagash Island, where you built a life for yourself. But in the process, you buried those nightmare sights and sounds." He gave a faint smile. "Time to resurrect them, that's all I'm saying."

He gazed down at her, wishing he could banish the same images: a raised gun, a bleeding dog, a terrified teenager running for her life through dark, garbage-strewn alleys. He had the feeling they'd be with him for the rest of his life. He was also, he realized, seething with anger. At a world that allowed such things to happen. At Del, for not making any effort to track Tess down when she was young and in desperate need. At himself, because six years ago he hadn't been there for her, hadn't even known she existed.

She could have gone under so easily, and been forever lost. He couldn't let the anger out now: it was the worst of times. He put his arm around Tess's waist. "Right now, let's call it quits," he said. "You've done more than enough for one night."

It was a measure of her tiredness that she made no argument. Keeping his emotions under tight rein, Cade walked her back to the house; and chose her bedroom, rather than his, for her to spend the rest of the night. With impersonal briskness he undressed her, found a nightgown in her drawer and pulled the covers over her. But before she closed her eyes, she reached for his hand and pressed it to her lips. "Thank you," she whispered. Still clasping his fingers, she fell into a stunned sleep.

But Cade stayed awake, sitting beside the bed. Keeping vigil, he thought soberly, as darkness faded from the sky and the first birds began to sing in the tall trees.

He should never have started this affair. Tess had been damaged more than enough in her short life, without him adding to it. His affairs were always short-lived. Worse, this particular one was with the woman who was Del's granddaughter; he, Cade, would have an ongoing relationship with her for the rest of his life, whether he wanted to or not. Avoiding her totally would be impossible.

He'd been an idiot in Venice, thinking with his hormones, not his brain cells. He should have sent her straight back to her room in her virginal-white gown.

Damage control, he thought heavily. How was he going to accomplish that?

One thing he could do, tangential though it was. He could confront Del with Cory's chequered past, and ask why Cory's existence had been kept a secret. Ask, too, why Del had never tried to contact Tess. It was due time for those ghosts to be laid to rest.

As for him, he'd better start keeping Tess at arm's length. Arm's length? he thought with vicious irony. He should end the affair right now, before any more damage was done.

Which meant that never again would he hold her in his arms, naked, breathtakingly beautiful, so generous she made nonsense of any concept of distance...

When Tess woke up, she was alone in her bedroom. It was sixteen minutes past midday.

The events of last night crowded into her mind. In a barn in Kentucky, she'd broken one of her inviolable rules: never to tell anyone about the events of those terrible days after Cory died. But she'd told Cade. Nor, she thought, stretching the stiffness from her limbs, had the sky fallen.

She scrambled out of bed, showered and went downstairs

for lunch, hoping to find Cade there. However, she had the vast dining room to herself. A note and a flat package were sitting beside her plate, the handwriting on the envelope Cade's. She slit it open and quickly read the scrawled words. He'd had to go to Manhattan but he'd be back tomorrow in time for the ball. Zeke would give her riding lessons the next two days. The package had been delivered this morning and he hoped she'd wear the contents with her green dress. His signature was a slash of black ink: Cade.

No reason to feel uneasy. What had she expected, that he'd sign it *Love, Cade*? Or that he'd mention what had happened last night?

Eating a deliciously light omelet, she looked at the flat box suspiciously. She might not be sophisticated, but she recognized the name Tiffany's.

Open it, Tess. It's not going to bite you.

In the end, she took the package up to her room to open it in privacy. Anchored to a bed of soft white velvet, emeralds flashed green fire: a pendant with a single stone on a delicate gold chain; earrings with more emeralds dangling from tiny gold chains; a gold bracelet set with emeralds. She'd never in her life seen jewellry so beautiful.

Cade should be here. Why hadn't he waited to give them to her himself, tomorrow night? To circle her throat with the pendant, to kiss her nape…

How could she be so ungrateful as to be critical of him?

The uneasy feeling hadn't gone away; if anything, it had magnified. She shoved the slim leather box into her top drawer; mucking out stalls and pitchforking hay would improve her mood.

Cade didn't phone, that day or the next.

She shouldn't have told him about Amsterdam, Tess

thought sickly, as she twisted to do up the zipper on her green dress the second evening. Sure, he'd listened. But what choice had he had when she was blubbering all over him?

If only she could undo that scene in the barn.

Through the open window, she heard the sound of a car approaching. Gazing out, she watched a limo draw up in the circular driveway. Cade climbed out, carrying an overnight bag and a briefcase, and hurried to the front door.

Her hands were cold and her pulses racing. She was dreading the ball tonight, she realized, the speculative glances, the inevitable questions about her whereabouts for the last twenty-two years. She'd know only one person there—Cade—and she'd had exactly one dancing lesson in her entire life.

But she'd be adorned with a small fortune in emeralds, she thought with a spurt of anger.

Footsteps hurried along the hallway outside her room, passing her door. Cade's door shut with a crisp snap. Two minutes later she heard his shower start.

If she was half as brave as he claimed she was, she'd go to his room and offer to dry his back. He hadn't even taken the time to tap on her door, or to kiss her. It was as if she no longer existed.

By making love with him, she'd trusted him with her body. But by telling him about Jake and Hans, she'd trusted him with her soul.

Her thoughts marched on. The decision never to talk about Amsterdam wasn't just about repression; it was about self-preservation as well. She'd been smart to keep her past to herself. How many people wanted to associate with a woman who'd once been as homeless as a stray dog, on the run from drug dealers and gangs?

Obviously Cade didn't. He'd disappeared for two days and now he was ignoring her.

She'd told him once that anyone with a credit card could buy emeralds. The jewels lying in their velvet-lined case were indeed an empty gesture if he no longer respected her. If he no longer wanted her.

Or was there more going on than that?

Cold terror had uncoiled like a snake in her belly. Desperately she tried to smother it. She wasn't going to fall apart again, not twice in forty-eight hours. Once had been once too often.

You've done more than enough for one night…as clearly as if she was back in the barn, she heard Cade's words echo in her head. At the time, she'd taken them at face value. But now, they were more ambiguous.

He hadn't asked her to tell him the details about that past: he'd asked her to write them down for her own use. The difference was crucial.

He didn't want to know the details.

Her fingers ice-cold, Tess did up her thin-strapped gold sandals. Quickly she inserted the earrings into her lobes and fastened the bracelet around her wrist. But despite her best efforts she couldn't manage the clasp on the pendant. Then she sat down on her bed and waited.

The shower shut off. Five minutes later, she heard Cade's door close again, and a decisive tap came at her door. She stood up, drawing composure around her like a cloak.

"Come in," she said.

Cade strode into Tess's bedroom. She was standing very still, a slim, wary figure in a gold-embroidered dress that fit her like a glove. Tiny sparks of green shot from her earlobes and wrist. "Sorry I'm late," he said abruptly. "Are you ready?"

He looked formidably elegant in his tux, yet as untamed as the panther Tess had once compared him to. Neither had he, in her opinion, sounded overly sorry. She said with formal exactitude, "Thank you for the emeralds."

"*No hay de qué,*" he said, his touch of sarcasm grating on her nerves. "You're not wearing the pendant."

"I can't do up the clasp."

Cade looked at her in silence. Damage control, he thought. Keep your distance.

She hadn't taken a single step toward him; so his strategy was working. Now all he had to do was maintain it. Easy enough when he was in Manhattan and she was in Kentucky. Not so easy face-to-face with her, when she looked delicious enough to eat and was stationed scarcely two feet away from a very wide bed.

Clumsily for him, Cade lifted the pendant from its velvet bed—he had beds on the brain, he thought savagely—and looped it around her neck. As she bent her nape, his fingers brushed her skin; a shiver rippled through her. His jaw tightened. Fumbling with the small gold clasp, he fastened it and stepped back.

"I'm ready," she said.

Her spine was ramrod straight. Knowing better than to touch her, for if he did he'd be lost, Cade said, "We should go. It's a ten-mile drive." Then he heard himself add, "You're not a horse going to the glue factory, Tess—you're a beautiful woman going to a high-society shindig that lots of people would give their eyeteeth to attend."

"I'm not lots of people," she said crisply, and draped her gold shawl around her shoulders.

Yet another Maserati—a black one this time, she noticed—was parked outside waiting for them. Cade turned on the radio, effectively drowning out conversation, and drove fast along the dark, winding highway: fast enough that she didn't want to distract him. Or was that just an excuse for her silence?

As the shadowed fields and black silhouettes of trees flashed by, the pride that had sustained Tess through years of unfulfilling jobs and mean lodgings came to her rescue. Be damned if she'd beg for Cade's attention, or fall all over him because he'd given her a few pretty green baubles. Let his other women do that. She wasn't going to.

But her nerves, she knew, were stretched to the breaking point; and as Cade drove along an *allée* of live oaks toward a mansion whose every window gleamed with light, they tightened another notch.

If she could sleep wrapped in cardboard, she could face a roomful of strangers. Cade pulled up by the wide arch of steps and turned off the ignition. "I'll stick with you," he said briefly. "And if they play a rhumba, I'll make sure no one else asks you to dance."

"Too bad I have such a limited repertoire," she said, her green eyes flashing; she was, she realized, spoiling for a fight. "I can always head for the powder room—I'm sure you'll find someone else to dance the rhumba with you."

"I'm sure I could," he grated, got out of the car and opened her door.

They climbed the steps side by side, between an array of antique pots full of scented camellias, and were ushered in the massive oak door by a uniformed butler. A middle-aged couple bustled toward them, the woman plump in yellow satin, her husband plumper in a tux with a bright yellow cummerbund. "Cade, darling," the woman exclaimed. "And this must be Del's granddaughter—you have his eyes, honey. Wasted on a man, I always said. I'm Bee Alden, and this is

my husband, Chuck." She leaned forward and kissed Tess on
the cheek. "Welcome to *Belle Maison*."

Chuck said, "Tess, you're a whole lot prettier than Del ever
was. Now you be sure to save me a waltz or two. Bee's been
at me for years, but seems like a waltz is the only dance where
I don't tramp all over my partner's feet."

Tess chuckled. "I'd be delighted to. We could even risk a
foxtrot—I'm good at dodging."

"Well now, aren't you a sweetheart?" Chuck said. "Cade,
good to see you, boy. Why don't you take your pretty lady
inside and get her a glass of bubbly? Soon as the guests stop
arriving, honey, I'll be right along to claim you."

As they passed out of earshot, Cade said softly, "Bee wears
a different color satin every year with her hair dyed to match,
and she's got the kindest heart in the south. Ah…now this
couple, they'll give you the third-degree."

A couple as disapproving as the ancestral portraits at
Cypress Acres was walking toward them, the woman's thin
lips coated with what was no doubt Dior lipstick. Tess tensed,
then soon discovered she'd scarcely needed to. With a skill
she had to admire, Cade fielded questions that were more than
pointed and observations that verged on bitchy. Then he
whisked her away to meet a white-maned senator who'd gone
to college with Del.

One by one, the expensively dressed guests paraded past
her, openly curious, overly tactful or—rather more than she'd
expected—just plain friendly. She waltzed with Cade, with
Chuck and with the senator; and gradually she relaxed. She
couldn't fault Cade's behavior; he was taking every measure
he could to ensure she enjoyed herself, and his physical close-
ness as they danced together set her heart to singing. As they
filled their plates at a buffet so colorful, so enticing that she

forgot everything in pure delight, she heard herself laughing and chatting as though she'd been attending society funtions all her life.

Amsterdam was another world.

Where had that thought come from? Tess shoved it away as she helped herself to tiny rolls of puff pastry stuffed with shrimp and avocado. Amsterdam was in the past. Over. Done with.

The contrast between this world and that was too cruel.

She took another gulp of champagne, bubbles tickling her nostrils. After they'd eaten, Cade led her onto the dance floor again; his steel-hard muscles under his formal jacket brought a flush to her cheeks, a liquid grace to her movements. Eyes shining, lips parted, she abandoned herself to the sheer pleasure of being in his arms.

But then the band struck up a Latin rhythm, catchy and sensual. She said, smiling up at him, "The powder room—I'll be back in a minute."

"I'll keep an eye out for you," he said.

It wasn't the moment to remember how, at dawn two mornings ago, those same eyes had roamed from the rosy tips of her breasts to her writhing hips, his big body hovering over her. Blushing, she mumbled, "Won't be long."

The powder room wouldn't have been out of place in a DelMer hotel, for it boasted gold-framed mirrors, fragrant bouquets of freesias, and a luxurious array of creams, soaps and linen hand towels. Trying not to gape, Tess discovered a small sitting room off the bathroom, wallpapered in the same heavy brocade, and tucked herself in one corner. Easing off her sandals, she decided to repair her lipstick and take some breathing space before she went back to the ballroom.

The outside door opened. A well-bred voice said languidly, "Del Lorimer's granddaughter is a pretty little thing."

Tess froze to her seat. "Marcia," a younger voice replied, "the gal's a raving beauty. Head over heels in love with Cade, of course."

"Naïve of her to be so obvious about it," the languid voice replied. "Someone should warn her. Won't be any wedding bells in that direction, Caro."

Caro sighed. "If I was twenty years younger and forty pounds lighter, I'd be in love with him, too."

"Wouldn't get you anywhere, darling," Marcia drawled. "Cade's not the marrying type. Pity. All those lovely greenbacks."

"You remember Talia Banks?—she's here somewhere with her latest man. She had an affair with him a year or so ago. Generous to a fault, she said, but he called the shots."

"Guess that's how you end up a billionaire…shall we go back? What *do* you think of Bee's hair?"

Caro sniggered. "I'm waiting for the year she chooses turquoise satin."

"Darling, really…"

The door closed behind them. Tess let out her pent-up breath, deeply thankful they hadn't checked out the sitting room. With some difficulty, because her fingers were trembling, she did up her gold shoes. *In love with Cade.*

Head over heels in love with Cade…

CHAPTER THIRTEEN

SHE was in love with Cade, Tess thought. Of course she was. The truth had been staring her in the face for days, but it had taken two gossipy socialites to make it sink in. Happiness rose like sunlight within her, brilliantly bright and warm. How astonishing, she thought. How amazing! She, Tess Ritchie, had fallen in love with a man so handsome, so sexy, that he turned her bones to water.

She had no idea when it had happened—so gradually she hadn't noticed, or very suddenly in the barn when she'd sobbed all over him. Did it matter?

Her reflection in one of the mirrors was staring back at her, a radiant smile on its face; her heart was racing as though she'd been waltzing for thirty minutes nonstop. Hastily she took her lipstick from her gold evening bag and slicked it over her mouth, trying to subdue the smile. She couldn't hide here forever. But how was she going to face Cade knowing that she loved him?

You've always had secrets, she told herself. This is a happy one, for a change. But it's still your secret. Just pray he's not in intimate conversation with a woman twenty years too old and forty pounds overweight whose name is Caro.

She ran a brush through her hair and walked back into the ballroom. The band was playing a tango, music so aggressively sexual that her steps slowed. She saw Cade immediately. He was dancing with a tall, leggy brunette in a backless black dress, a sulty smile on her lips.

Dancing? He wasn't dancing. He was publicly making love to her. Dipping her backward, whirling her in circles, pulling her toward him only to thrust her away.

An untamed mix of fury and knife-sharp pain ripped through Tess's body, red-hot, ice-cold. Cade, who had promised to watch out for her, had totally forgotten her.

The brunette didn't have a limited repertoire.

So this, Tess thought, was jealousy. The dark side of love, its ugly sister. Although she'd never felt it before, she knew what it was instantly. She wanted to tear the brunette from Cade's arms. She wanted to run for the door and keep running until she was—where? Where could she run? For Cade was everywhere, and wherever she ran, she'd carry him with her.

And that, too, was love.

The band ended on a triumphant chord. Cade had whipped the brunette into his chest and was holding her to his body. He was laughing.

Bee said briskly, "Now, honey, you mustn't wear your heart on those cute cap sleeves of yours for everyone to see. Here, have some more bubbly. I always say to Chuck that there isn't a trouble invented a glass of champagne can't fix."

Numbly Tess took the proffered crystal flute. "I'm in love with him," she blurted.

"Of course you are. Who wouldn't be? Just because I'm happily married doesn't mean I can't admire the finest set of pecs this side of California. But, honey, I should warn you, marriage is a dirty word as far as Cade's concerned. His mother's divorce—messy, very messy. And then the custody battle—well, who can blame him for being gun-shy?"

"Custody battle?" Tess faltered. She'd always assumed that Selena, Cade's mother, had been a widow. Certainly Cade had never mentioned divorce.

Bee gave a sigh that was partly pleasurable. "What a spectacle it was—the country club dined off it for weeks. Cade's father didn't want Cade, never had—but he didn't want Selena having him, either. Well, the lawyers got rich, which is always the way, and in the end the judge voted for motherhood." She gave Tess a shrewd glance. "This is news to you? Cade's been closemouthed since he was a boy, with very good reason."

When had she, Tess, ever asked Cade about his real father, or what had happened to that father? She hadn't. She'd been too absorbed in her own troubles; and had, she thought guiltily, too easily jumped to the conclusion that Cade, so rich, so handsome, so accomplished, had no real troubles of his own other than a less-than-close relationship with Del.

So two fathers hadn't wanted Cade: his biological father and his adoptive father. The mystery that was Cade was suddenly clearer to Tess. No wonder commitment was a dirty word to him. A double-edged rejection had scarred him for life, marked him so deeply that he wouldn't allow himself to need her, or be needed by her.

To love or be loved.

"There now," Bee said, "Cade's looking for you. Off you go, honey, and take my advice—play your cards close to your emeralds."

Tess gave an involuntary gulp of laughter that was all too close to tears. "Thanks, Bee," she said, and started across the room toward Cade. The brunette had vanished. He was standing at the edge of the dance floor, watching her approach, waiting for her. Out of duty?

In spite of herself, anger was hot in her breast again. She'd told Cade the sordid story of her past; but had he confided in her? No, sir.

Anger was preferable to swooning at his feet because she'd been stupid enough to fall in love with him. Or bursting into tears because he'd never marry her.

Marriage, she thought blankly. She was the woman who'd said—fairly adamantly, as she recalled—that she never wanted to marry anyone.

She'd changed her mind. A total about-face. But would Cade ever change his?

He said curtly, "You were gone a long time."

"You managed to entertain yourself while I was gone."

"Talia asked me to dance."

Her heart clenched in her chest. "An old friend?" she said silkily.

"She and I were lovers a year or so ago," he said impatiently. "I'm only telling you before you hear it from someone else."

A devil had control of her tongue. "So we've had Sharon and now Talia. Are we working our way down the alphabet?"

"If I didn't know you better, I'd say you were jealous."

"You know me very well. In bed, at least."

"Tess," he said with treacherous gentleness, "if you want to have a knock-em-down fight, I'll be happy to oblige. But not here and not now."

A headache was brewing behind her eyes. "I wish I'd never left Malagash Island," she said with the truth of desperation. "Never met you!"

"You've done both," he said brusquely. "The senator wants you to meet his brother and sister-in-law—they have a summer place in Maine. Come along."

For a moment she contemplated marching straight out of the ballroom into the cool, star-spangled night: that would really set the tongues wagging, and not just in the powder room. The thought cheered her up somewhat; and the senator's family turned out to be as charming as the senator.

Dancing with Cade, though, in what was only a facade of intimacy, was more painful than Tess would have believed possible. She couldn't bear for him to guess that she was in love with him; when, briefly, she was introduced to a group that included Talia, she kept her poise by sheer force of will. But her headache worsened; a dull throbbing had settled behind her eyes, interspersed with sudden sharp flashes of pain.

As he took her onto the dance floor in yet another waltz, Cade said evenly, "What's wrong?"

"I have a headache."

"Why didn't you say so? I'll take you home."

To her own bed at Cypress Acres. Alone. Because she would use the headache, Tess thought with unhappy truth; the other thing she didn't dare do was make love with Cade, knowing that she loved him. In the intimacy of his big bed, how could she possibly disguise her feelings? "Sounds good," she said in careful understatement.

Ten minutes later, they were accelerating down the driveway under the dark canopy of trees. "Do you have any aspirin?" Cade said.

"No. I never get headaches."

"Why tonight? You were a great success."

The words escaped in spite of herself. "What have you got against marriage, Cade?"

He glanced over at her, his eyes hooded. "I already told you—a high potential for boredom."

"Nothing to do with your parents' custody battle?"

His fingers tensed on the wheel. "Who told you about that?"

"Not you."

"Why would I?"

Hurt slammed through her. So love was also vulnerability, she thought, and said carefully, "I told you about Jake and Hans."

He said flatly, "My father insisted on a cold, businesslike marriage that would advance his medical career and give my mother plenty of time for volunteer work. Then she met Del and, I suppose, discovered what she'd been missing. She filed for divorce, my father hired the shark-lawyer-of-the-year, and the fight was on."

"You were a pawn in that fight."

"She impoverished herself in the courts," he said harshly. "But she stuck with it, and she won. End of story."

"Beginning of story, I'd say, if you've been running from marriage ever since...Cade, I'm so sorry I never asked. I always assumed Selena was a widow."

"She and Del were good together. But The Rose Room at Moorings says it all—at heart, my mother was a conventional woman. They were settled. Comfortable. Content." Unconsciously he was banging his fist on the wheel. "If that's all there is, I'd rather stay single."

"You and I aren't like that."

"Lust, Tess. It'll burn out. It always does."

"And what if it doesn't? Are you still going to run away?"

"Dammit," he exploded, "it's not that simple. You're Del's granddaughter, I'm responsible for you."

"I'm responsible for myself!"

"I don't care if this sounds arrogant," he said. "I'm worried if we continue our affair you'll get in too deep."

"You're afraid I'll fall in love with you," she said with deadly accuracy, and watched him nod. "What if I already have?"

"Don't play games."

"What if I asked you to marry me? What would you say?"

Abruptly he pulled over to the side of the road, and turned in his seat to face her, his eyes burning into hers. "Am I missing something here? What the hell's going on?"

"Answer my question."

"I'd say no."

In spite of herself, she flinched. "Just like that."

"Tess, you're not in love with me. In less than three weeks, you've been lifted out of a backwater island, presented with a new grandfather and thrust into high society. It's no surprise that—"

"You left something out," she said icily. "I also lost my virginity. Or had you forgotten?"

"I should never have started this affair! When you knocked on my door in Venice, I should have sent you back to your room. I was the one with experience—and I don't care what you say, I was the one responsible for you."

"But you didn't send me back," she said softly and knew at some deep level that she was fighting for her life. "I'm the woman who makes you break the rules. Who destroys your control, who drives you out of your mind—and now I'm the one who's sounding arrogant. Cade, do you seriously think you and I would have a boring marriage? Or that we'd ever use our children as pawns even if we did divorce?"

"For God's sake—one more reason I'm against marriage is so I'll never have to go anywhere near a divorce lawyer."

"Was your father a good man? A loving man?"

"Neither. He was cold-blooded, selfish and manipulative." The words forced from him, he added, "I've never ceased being grateful to my mother for not abandoning me to him all those years ago."

"You're a good man at heart," Tess said passionately. "You love Del, I know you do, in spite of the fact he's always held himself aloof from you. You're different from your father. As different as you could be."

"Since when did you get to be such an authority?"

"Since you first took me into your bed. I may be inexperienced, but some things can't be faked. Your care for me, your generosity, your passion—they're you. Your essence."

She was leaning forward, speaking with the intensity that was so characteristic of her. The sweet rise of her breasts above her embroidered bodice clawed Cade with desire; the single emerald was swinging gently in her cleavage, shooting green sparks. When he'd chosen the pendant, hadn't he pictured making love to her with it as her only adornment? Right now, he ached to take her in his arms, to end this ridiculous discussion the only way he knew how.

She *was* in danger of falling in love with him. Tonight had proved it. And there was another way to end the discussion. A brutal way, yes—but brutally effective. Not stopping to think, because if he did he might back off, Cade said, "When we started the affair, we made an agreement—when the time came to end it, we'd do it up-front. That time's come, Tess. I'm ending it. Now. My only regret is starting it in the first place."

She shrank back in her seat. "You regret making love with me?" she faltered.

"That's not what I meant."

"That's what it sounded like!"

"In Adelaide and Venezuela we'll act as business associates only," he said, biting off the words. "After that, you're on your own—I'll keep out of your way at Moorings, or wherever else you choose to go."

Clutching straws, she said, "What about Del?"

"If you're wise, you'll never tell Del we've been involved."

"As though I'm ashamed of the most beautiful thing that's ever happened to me?"

"Because it's none of his business!"

"Keep everything compartmentalized," she said bitterly. "That's how you've always lived, isn't it? Sex over here, business over there and no place for feelings."

"I'll live my life the way I choose. Right now I'm ending our affair before I do more harm than I've already done. It's not open for negotiation—my mind's made up."

As suddenly as he'd stopped the car, Cade swung back on the highway. The Maserati surged forward into the darkness. Tess leaned back on the cool leather and closed her eyes, her hands clenched in her lap. Other than confessing she'd fallen in love with Cade, and begging him to marry her, what more could she say? She'd fought for her life—for her newly discovered love—and she'd lost. The Venetian Affair had just come to an end on a country road in Kentucky.

Into her mind dropped the image of her little cabin by the sea. She was going back there, she thought desperately. As soon as she could. Del could visit her there, if he chose to. But she was through dancing to Cade's tune.

Her headache was a vicious, throbbing reality, as though a dozen rock bands were tuning up inside her skull. All she wanted was to be alone—so that for the second time in as many nights she could cry her eyes out.

But not yet. She had too much pride to show Cade how deeply he'd hurt her.

The drive home seemed to last forever; as she followed Cade up the front steps at Cypress Acres, she was swaying with fatigue. He said tightly, "I've acted for the best tonight, Tess. You don't agree with me now, but in time you will."

"Don't try to control my feelings," she seethed. "You may

be a billionaire, but if you won't risk falling in love with me, you might as well be poverty-stricken."

His fingers dug into her elbow. "That's ludicrous and you know it."

"Let go of me," she said with iciness of true rage. "You don't want to have an affair with me—so I'm off-limits. No touching allowed."

Her skin was cool, and silken-smooth. He was right to end the affair, he knew he was. Yet all he wanted to do was pull Tess into his arms and kiss her senseless. Cade dropped her elbow, matching her rage with his own. "You're assuming I want to touch you."

"Go back to Talia. Or Sharon. But leave me alone," she said and pushed open the door. To her infinite relief, Cade didn't follow her up the stairs. Alone in her own bedroom at last, she locked the door and leaned back on the panels. But her eyes were dry, burning in their sockets.

She kicked off her gold sandals, stepped out of her dress and flung the emerald earrings and bracelet on the dresser. However, once again, she couldn't manage the clasp on her pendant. Swearing under her breath, she left it dangling around her neck, and grabbed the least sexy of her nightgowns.

Then she stationed herself on the window seat overlooking the paddock and the gently rising hills, leaned against the cold glass and waited for night to be over.

At seven the next morning, Tess threw on a pair of jeans and started downstairs. Her plan was to go to the barn. For comfort, she thought, and as she turned the corner saw with a stab of pure agony that Cade was standing in the foyer. Cade and his overnight bag.

With all her willpower, she forced herself to continue her

descent. Then he glanced up, caught sight of her and took a step toward her. She froze on the bottom step.

He said choppily, "I'm heading to Maine for a couple of days—I want to see Del. Best thing is for you to stay here."

Her decision was instant. "I'm coming with you."

"Tess, you're not—"

"You're through running my life," she said frigidly. "I have to see Del, too. He's my grandfather, and he's not well."

Cade said reluctantly, "So it's not a charade anymore—you and Del."

She let out her breath in a small sigh. "He meant nothing to me initially, I was being honest when I told you that…and he's not the rock to cling to that I needed so desperately when I was small. But he shares my blood, and in his obstinate way he's trying to do right by me." In spite of herself, her voice shook. "I can't turn my back on him—he's all I've got."

"He needs you as much as you need him," Cade said harshly.

"He needs you, too."

"Don't kid yourself. He told me the day he married my mother that he didn't want me to call him Dad. Ever. I was only eight, but I knew there was a message there. Del doesn't need me. He never has."

Frowning, Tess said slowly, "Cory must have caused him so much grief…perhaps he couldn't let you close because he was afraid of being hurt all over again."

Cade's gut clenched. Of course. It was so blindingly obvious that he hadn't seen it. Cory would have broken Del's heart over and over again. Why wouldn't Del keep his adoptive son at a distance?

The look on Cade's face stabbed Tess to the core. "Maybe it's time to ask Del why he wouldn't let you near. If it really was self-protection."

Cade wasn't about to make any promises, to her or to himself. "If you're coming with me, Tess, you'd better hurry."

Once again Cade had retreated, his face a tight mask. Tess said briefly, "Give me five minutes to pack my bags."

She ran upstairs, past the disapproving ancestors, and dragged her suitcase out of the closet. Leaving the elegant green gown on its hanger because she never wanted to see it again, she flung in some of her more casual clothes and changed into an uncrushable silk pantsuit. Hastily she tucked the emerald pendant beneath her camisole and snapped the case shut.

In a few hours she'd be back in Maine. She'd go to Malagash Island; and this time she wouldn't leave.

She hurried downstairs. Cade was waiting for her in the car. After she'd slammed her door, he put his foot to the accelerator. In a voice devoid of feeling, he said, "The cook filled the thermos with coffee and there are a couple of freshly baked Danish in the box."

"The cook deserves a medal," Tess replied and put on her dark glasses, ostensibly against the early morning sun, in actuality to hide from Cade. She was hungry, she realized in faint surprise, and poured herself a mug of steaming coffee. In between chewing apricot croissants and taking naps to catch up on her sleep, she kept up a patter of light conversation during the journey: for which she herself deserved a medal, she thought derisively. But she was damned if she was going to let Cade know that he'd broken her heart.

What a trite phrase. Yet her rib cage felt sore, her muscles ached from tension and a cold knot had lodged itself in her belly. Unromantic symptoms, but all too real.

She'd tell Del her plans tonight, and tomorrow she'd go home to Malagash.

Once again, it would be the haven she'd always needed.

CHAPTER FOURTEEN

SEVERAL hours later, Cade pulled up in front of Moorings. He said tersely, "I'll go see Del first. When it's your turn, don't upset him."

It had been a long day. Tess said flippantly, "No, Mr. Lorimer."

He turned in his seat, his gray eyes turbulent. "Do you think it's easy, ending our affair when all I want to do is haul you off to the nearest bed? But I'm doing the right thing, I know I am. So quit making snide remarks!"

"If it's that difficult, why is it the right thing?"

He seized her by the shoulders, planted a furious kiss full on her mouth, then pushed her away. "The butler will bring your case in," he snarled. "I won't be with Del for very long."

Inside the house, Cade took the stairs two at a time. Hastily he scrubbed at his mouth before he tapped on the door; the last thing he needed was lipstick smeared on his face.

As he walked in Del's room, the old man's face changed. "Thought you were the doc. Got me on a new medication, seems to be doing wonders. But he insists I sit around like a broody hen half the day."

"Then maybe you should listen," Cade said. His voice tight, he added, "I need to talk to you."

"Talk all you like. I got time."

There was no point in subtlety. "Through spending time with Tess, I've come to understand what a huge grief to you Cory must have been, Del. Is that why you were so reluctant to take on a second son? And why you never wanted me calling you Dad?"

"He nearly destroyed me," Del said harshly. "From the time he was a little boy, he was dishonest, aggressive and casually cruel. I couldn't fathom him or tolerate him. Couldn't make him change his ways, either. When I divorced his mother—my first wife—for adultery, the two of them took off to Europe, and good riddance. After she died a few years later, Cory contacted me for money." Del shrugged. "I paid him off on the condition he stay in Europe. And once Tess was born, I sent a monthly allowance. Well, we know what happened to that."

"You didn't try to see her," Cade said stiffly.

Del passed his hand over his face; he looked, Cade thought in compunction, every year of his age. "I never told Selena just how bad Cory was. Thought she'd quit loving me if she knew I had a rotten egg for a son. So I couldn't tell her about Tess, either. I loved your mother, Cade, but I never really understood why she loved me."

"You didn't think you deserved her," Cade said in sudden enlightenment.

"That's about it. So I kept it all a secret—and Tess is the one who suffered, along with you. Because you're dead on— I kept you at a distance on purpose. I'm sorry, Cade. More sorry than I can say."

It was as though a great weight he'd scarcely been aware of carrying had lifted from his chest. Cade said slowly, "If you're willing, it's not too late to bridge the gap."

Del cleared his throat. "Yeah, I'm willing."

"Tess has done us a good turn," Cade said huskily.

"She's okay, is Tess." Del sat up straight. "So what do you think of the latest vote in congress?"

With alacrity, Cade dove into the murky field of politics, an area where he and Del had never seen eye to eye. Half an hour later, he went to his office to check his faxes from Los Angeles; he was planning to fly there tomorrow, put some space between him and Tess.

There'd be no Venezuelan Affair. Let alone Australian, Asian or Argentinian.

Early the next morning, Del's chauffeur left Tess at the top of her driveway on Malagash Island. Fog had rolled in during the night. Waves washed softly onto the beach, rattling the pebbles. A gull mewed eerily.

She started down the slope; and knew that with every step she took, Cade was flying further and further away from her, on his way to Los Angeles. *Pressing business,* he'd said. *A good time to put a little distance between us.*

Startling her, a crow cawed from its perch on a piece of ghost-white driftwood. She'd slept badly, and had spent the black hours of night trying to convince herself that she was confusing lust with romance, and sex with love. It hadn't worked. She loved Cade, irrevocably.

Unrequited love was another cliché, she thought miserably, digging in her purse for her house keys. How was she to live with it, day after day? Where would she find the resolve to get up in the morning?

The cabin smelled musty and unlived in. Her plants had died from lack of water, and a storm had crusted the windows with salt spray. Why had she never realized how small the cabin was?

She shivered, trailing into her bedroom, where she'd slept alone so happily, content to hear the tides rise and fall and the seabirds cry. It, too, felt claustrophobically small.

She should open a few windows, cycle to the store, get some food in. Instead she walked out onto the deck, the deck where she'd served Cade coffee and homemade muffins on a morning that now seemed a lifetime ago. The fog was cool on her cheeks, dampening her hair.

The other man she loved was, of course, Del. *Gramps,* she'd called him on their last couple of visits, not realizing the name was concealing true affection. But when she'd seen him yesterday, caged in his room like a ruffled old eagle, she'd understood how much he meant to her.

Love, in two very different guises, had trapped her. She couldn't run off to a château in France and make a new life for herself thousands of miles from Cade; she needed to be closer to Del.

Close to Del meant close to Cade.

Trapped, indeed. In the last three weeks, her world had expanded its boundaries immeasurably. From Manhattan to Madrid, from hotels and gondoliers to horse barns and vineyards, she'd discovered a whole new existence; and in Cade's arms, she'd found a fulfillment that had drenched her in intimacy.

She couldn't go back to the life she'd known on the island, she thought, gazing into the thick folds of fog. It was too late. She'd outgrown her little cabin.

Yet, at this precise moment, she had no idea what was to replace it.

As though the fog had shifted, clearing the view, she suddenly remembered herself as a little girl, the day she fell off the red swing at the playground. She'd scraped her knee;

it had oozed a nasty mixture of blood and gravel. She'd run for her nanny, knowing that Bella would hold her and comfort her, and the pain would go away...

That's what I'll do, Tess thought. *I'll go to Madrid and see Ysabel. She'll understand. Maybe, just maybe, she can tell me what to do next.*

Quickly she fumbled in her pocket for the chauffeur's cell phone number. If Cade could fly west, she could fly east.

Perhaps he was right, and distance was what she needed.

Cade got back to Moorings the next day. With immense reluctance, he stared up at Del's seaside mansion. Tess was inside. In a few moments, he'd have to face her.

He'd driven himself—and his employees—into the ground in Los Angeles. It hadn't helped. Day and night, he'd been saturated with Tess's absence: darkness, of course, far worse than daylight.

Withdrawal symptoms, Cade thought with vicious emphasis, as he mounted the front steps. He'd gone from a heavy dose of the most amazing sex in his life to none at all. No wonder he was sleeping badly.

Inside, the dogs greeted him with wild enthusiasm; then the butler handed him a note. "From Miss Ritchie," he said. "And Mr. Lorimer would like to see you before he settles for the night."

In the privacy of his room, Cade tore open the envelope and read the brief message.

By the time you get this, I'll be in Madrid with Ysabel. Then I may go to Amsterdam. You're right, Cade, we need to put distance between us. Tess.

He should be relieved that he didn't have to face her, that she'd gotten the message that his way was the right way. The only way.

He wasn't.

Madrid was bad enough, Cade thought furiously. But Tess, alone, in Amsterdam? What was she thinking?

He was going after her. Amsterdam was, for her, a city of nightmares, and be damned if she was going to face them on her own.

So much for distance, a little voice sneered in his ear.

Shut up, he snarled, went to the phone and made a couple of calls. Then he unpacked and repacked, showered and had a brief visit with Del: a visit during which he determinedly confined the conversation to matters of business.

Several hours later, Cade was standing in the lobby of Madrid's DelMer Hotel talking to the receptionist. "Tess Ritchie," he said, his voice gravelly from jet lag. "She hasn't checked out, has she?"

"No, sir. She's checking out tomorrow morning. Let me call her room."

Although Tess didn't answer, Cade at least knew she wasn't in Amsterdam. He ordered a cab, and went straight to Ysabel's apartment. Ysabel opened the door. Her accent more pronounced than usual, she said, "Cade—I wasn't expecting to see *you*."

Cade stepped inside, his eyes sweeping the small, cluttered room. "I'm looking for Tess."

Ysabel stepped back. "Why?"

Her voice was far from friendly, and she wasn't asking him to sit down. He said flatly, "To go to Amsterdam with her."

"She's not caught in your—how do you say?—apron ties. She's a grown woman, and your affair with her is over."

"So she told you that."

"It's not your business what she tells me."

"I couldn't risk her falling in love with me, Ysabel!"

Ysabel's magnificent dark eyes flashed. "Love isn't a disease. It's what makes us human."

He wasn't in the mood for a sermon. "Fine," he said. "Where is she?"

"You've come a long way to see her."

"Where *is* she?" he repeated, holding tight to his temper. "I have to talk to her."

"She left here two hours ago to go back to her hotel."

"On foot?"

"Of course. It wasn't then dark."

"She's not at the hotel," Cade rapped.

"Then she's gone into a bar to hear flamenco. Or into a restaurant for…" she fumbled for the word "—*la merienda*…the snack. I suggest you go back to the hotel and wait for her." Ysabel straightened to her full height. "If you hurt her again, you will have me on your coattails—you understand?"

"I never intended to hurt her," he said roughly.

"Then you should have been more careful of her heart."

Cade stood still, the truth hitting like a blow. "So she has fallen in love with me."

"That is for you to find out."

He said abruptly, "She was very fortunate that you were in her life when she was so young—thank you, Ysabel, for all that you've done for her." He then wheeled on the faded carpet and let himself out, running down the stairs and emerging onto the street.

Under orange awnings, couples were seated on the sidewalk, drinking beer and *vino tinto*. Music rollicked from a nearby *taberna*. Taking out his cell phone, Cade called the hotel; but Tess still wasn't in her room. He began to walk, trying to picture the route she'd take, his eyes darting back and forth across the heavy traffic; the whole time he was reining in an anxiety that would cripple him if he allowed it to.

Once he thought he saw her: a chestnut-haired woman with her back to him in a bar, eating *tapas* and laughing at something the man next to her had just said. His heart contracted with a hot pang of what was unquestionably jealousy; but when the woman turned her head, he saw she was older than Tess and nowhere near as beautiful.

Tess was entirely free to spend her time with whomever she wished. Or, he thought savagely, to take another man to her bed.

He crossed a busy square, taxis honking their horns, a policeman watching the chaos with a bored eye. Then, from two streets over, he heard sirens wailing; he turned down the street as though the sound was a magnet, his pulse racing. A truck was veered to one side with its hood badly dented, while a small sedan was crushed against a lamppost. Serious enough, but nothing to do with Tess.

What if it had been? What if that were her body being loaded into the back door of the ambulance?

What if, what if? What the devil was wrong with him?

She was a woman alone at night in a city that had the usual quota of crimes, large and small. He couldn't bear not knowing where she was or whether she was safe.

It was no longer anxiety cruising his nerves; it was fear.

An unruly gang of punks surged along the sidewalk toward him. Young males, high on testosterone and drugs, carelessly and loudly aggressive in their studded black leather and dangling chains. Cade knew from experience that in a flash they could change to something much more dangerous.

A straggler, obviously drunk, bumped into Cade; to his

overwrought imagination, the man could easily have been Hans, the gang leader who'd threatened her life seven years ago. "Get away from me," Cade snarled, adrenaline racing through his veins, his fists bunched at his sides. He knew any number of nasty moves from his two years of roughing it; if he had to, he'd use them.

Something must have shown in his face; the punk staggered off, belching. Cade straightened, his muscles taut in a ferocious mixture of aggression and rage.

If anything happened to Tess tonight, he'd never forgive himself.

Because he loved her.

No, he didn't, he thought wildly. He wasn't in love with anyone. And knew the words for a lie as soon as they'd flashed across his brain.

He, Cade Lorimer, had fallen in love with the green-eyed, fiery-tempered woman who'd turned his life upside down.

For a moment, all his other emotions were submerged in pure amazement at the simplicity, the rightness of a truth that was dazzlingly obvious. He stepped to one side of the pavement, the crowds eddying in around him. His jealousy, his mounting fear, his increasingly desperate search for her on the busy streets of a Spanish city, were all clues he'd ignored.

He had to find her. Tell her. Take her in his arms and make love to her the night through.

Providing she'd have him.

He couldn't go there. Not now.

Cade took off down the pavement at a fast clip. It took him thirty minutes to reach the hotel. Its baroque facade and decorated columns mocked him with their solidity; until he found Tess, nothing in the world was solid.

He marched into the lobby and phoned her room, hearing

a shrill, repetitive ringing until the voice mail clicked on. Then he checked the bar and the lounge. His last stop was the dining room, paneled in ornately carved mahogany, with tropical plants creating small oases of privacy among the scattered, gloriously hued Moroccan carpets.

At the far end, tucked into a corner table, Tess was having dinner. A book was open in front of her. She was absorbed in it, absently sipping a glass of *vino rosado*.

She looked as if she didn't have a care in the world.

Suddenly enraged beyond any bounds of common sense, Cade strode the length of the room, bamboo brushing his shoulders, the occasional waiter skipping nimbly out of his path. He came to a halt beside her table. "You look very much at home," he said.

The book slipped from her fingers, knocking over a silver dish filled with elaborate curls of butter. "Cade!" she gasped, pushing back her chair and scrambling to her feet. "What are you doing here?" Then she paled. "Del—he's had another heart attack?"

"Del's fine."

"Then what—"

"Tell me you're happy to see me," he said hoarsely.

Her chin snapped up. "Why should I? You ended our affair as casually as if—as if you were tossing aside a book you'd read."

"I was wrong. I made a mistake."

She swept on as though he hadn't spoken. "I came here to put distance between us. Distance that you insisted on, not me. So why are you here when I'm doing my best to forget about you?"

Her eyes were ablaze with fury; but around her neck, he saw the glimmer of a gold chain. "You're wearing the pendant I gave you."

"I can't undo the clasp," she retorted. "If you want it back, it's all yours."

"I want you to marry me," he said.

Her jaw dropped; she gripped the edge of the table as though it was all that was holding her up. "Are you out of your mind?"

"No," he said with a sudden feral grin. "I'm jet-lagged, I've been half-crazy with worry ever since I found out you'd left Ysabel's apartment three hours ago, and I nearly started a brawl on the sidewalk. I don't have a ring and I haven't composed any fancy speeches—so if you want diamonds and poetry, you're out of luck. But I do want you to marry me."

"Why? Because instead of chasing after you, I headed in the opposite direction?"

"Because I love you," he said.

Tess gaped at him. "This isn't happening…I'm dreaming and any minute I'm going to wake up all by myself in bed."

Cade took her in his arms, running his hands up and down her spine, then kissing her, sinking into the kiss until there was nothing else in the world but this one woman. With all her strength, Tess pushed him away. "Stop it! One day the affair's over, the next day you're kissing me as though there's no tomorrow?"

He said forcefully, "I want you today and tomorrow. Only you, and for all my tomorrows."

She was pummeling him on the chest. "I'll bore you. I'll make demands on you. I won't let your nasty, cold-blooded father run your life. You don't want me."

He captured her hands in his, gazing down into her furious eyes as he put all the conviction of his newfound love into his voice. "My body wants you, that hasn't changed. Never will. But my heart wants you, too. My heart and my soul. And they're what really count."

"Oh," she said, and he watched as fury was replaced by

an emotion he couldn't decipher. "That sounds sort of like poetry to me."

"I was a fool to end our affair. I was running scared, you were right. You were so different, you made nonsense of all my rules, and I didn't have a clue how to handle the way you made me feel."

"How do I make you feel?" Tess asked, knowing the question was all-important. In spite of herself, her hands crept up his chest, seeking the warmth and hardness of his body, so achingly familiar, so agonizingly missed.

"As though I was born to find you," he said hoarsely. "To need you and to love you. To marry you."

"You hated needing me," she said pithily. "It made you run in the opposite direction."

"I've stopped running," he said wryly. "About time, wouldn't you say?" He raked his fingers through his hair, searching for an argument that might persuade her, coming up with nothing but the strength of his own feelings. "Say you'll marry me. Or if you don't want marriage, that you'll at least live with me."

Her eyes narrowed. "There's something you're forgetting. Something crucial."

"Tell me what it is."

"You haven't asked how I feel about you."

"Hell, Tess, I'm scared to. I've done everything in my power the last few days to push you away—and now I'm supposed to ask if you love me?"

"You got the question right," Tess said with a sudden, radiant smile that caught at his heartstrings.

"So what's the answer?" he said roughly.

Finally she said the words she'd been longing to say for what felt like forever. "I do love you, Cade. I realized it at the ball, when I was skulking in the powder room—the very night you ended our affair." She bit her lip. "Terrible timing."

"I thought I was doing the right thing. For both of us. I've been wrong a few times in my life, but that night took the cake." He linked his arms around her waist. "Tell me again that you love me."

"I love you, love you, love you." Her smile broke out again. "And I'll do my best not to bore you."

"That's the least of our worries," Cade said, and kissed her again, a kiss fueled by a gratitude as deep and as passionate as his love; and this time he felt her yield. More than yield, he thought in a flood of joy, her response rocketing through him. "Marry me, Tess," he whispered against her lips. "I'll be as good to you as I know how, I swear I will. And I'll love you as long as there's breath in my body."

"I'll marry you, Cade."

"Even though you swore off marriage years ago?"

"If you can change your mind, I can change mine."

His own smile broke through. "I want you to wear white. Like the white you were wearing when you came to my room in Venice."

"We could honeymoon in Venice."

"A Venetian Marriage," he said huskily. "Sounds fine to me."

She gave a sudden ripple of laughter. "You won't be able to back out—we have a whole dining room full of witnesses."

"Then maybe I should order champagne all around, and ask everyone to charge their glasses to my future bride."

"Maybe you should."

So he did.

0508/06

MILLS & BOON

MODERN

On sale 6th June 2008

THE BILLIONAIRE BOSS'S SECRETARY BRIDE
by Helen Brooks

Fantastically rich and handsome Harry Breedon shows nothing
more than professional interest in reliable secretary Gina.
Or so she thinks! Now she's been offered another job,
he's determined to seduce her into staying…

THE GIANNAKIS BRIDE
by Catherine Spencer

Brianna Connelly holds the key to saving Dimitrios Giannakis'
daughter's life, though she refuses to let Dimitrios break
her heart again. Only the fierce chemistry between
them is as strong as ever…

DESERT KING, PREGNANT MISTRESS
by Susan Stephens

Sheikh Khalifa tires of the potential wives paraded in front
of him. Sweet, innocent Beth is a thrilling distraction! Arriving
at the island a naïve virgin, Beth leaves an awakened
woman – pregnant by the Sheikh…

RUTHLESS BOSS, HIRED WIFE
by Kate Hewitt

Powerful Cormac Douglas needs a temporary wife to secure a
prestigious contract, and biddable secretary Lizzie Chandler
is perfect! Lizzie is outraged, but Cormac's ruthless
persuasion leaves her breathlessly wanting more…

Celebrate 100 years of pure reading pleasure with Mills & Boon®

To mark our centenary, each month we're publishing a special 100th Birthday Edition. These celebratory editions are packed with extra features and include a FREE bonus story.

Plus, starting in February you'll have the chance to enter a fabulous monthly prize draw. See 100th Birthday Edition books for details.

Now that's worth celebrating!

15th February 2008

Raintree: Inferno by Linda Howard
Includes FREE bonus story Loving Evangeline
A double dose of Linda Howard's heady mix of passion and adventure

4th April 2008

The Guardian's Forbidden Mistress by Miranda Lee
Includes FREE bonus story The Magnate's Mistress
Two glamorous and sensual reads from favourite author Miranda Lee!

2nd May 2008

The Last Rake in London by Nicola Cornick
Includes FREE bonus story The Notorious Lord
Lose yourself in two tales of high society and rakish seduction!

Look for Mills & Boon 100th Birthday Editions at your favourite bookseller or visit
www.millsandboon.co.uk

0108/CENTENARY_2-IN-1

FREE

4 BOOKS AND A SURPRISE GIFT!

We would like to take this opportunity to thank you for reading this Mills & Boon® book by offering you the chance to take FOUR more specially selected titles from the Modern™ series absolutely FREE! We're also making this offer to introduce you to the benefits of the Mills & Boon® Reader Service™—

- ★ **FREE home delivery**
- ★ **FREE gifts and competitions**
- ★ **FREE monthly Newsletter**
- ★ **Books available before they're in the shops**
- ★ **Exclusive Reader Service offers**

Accepting these FREE books and gift places you under no obligation to buy; you may cancel at any time, even after receiving your free shipment. Simply complete your details below and return the entire page to the address below. You don't even need a stamp!

YES! Please send me 4 free Modern books and a surprise gift. I understand that unless you hear from me, I will receive 6 superb new titles every month for just £2.99 each, postage and packing free. I am under no obligation to purchase any books and may cancel my subscription at any time. The free books and gift will be mine to keep in any case.

P8ZEE

Ms/Mrs/Miss/Mr......................................Initials ....
BLOCK CAPITALS PLEASE

Surname ....

Address ....

....

....Postcode ....

Send this whole page to:
The Reader Service, FREEPOST CN81, Croydon, CR9 3WZ